TO: Kalena

Love in *Pictures*

By Alexis A. Goring

FROM:

May GOD bless you, your family, your work and your heart❤️ Love Alexis (author)

ISBN-13: 978-1-946939-87-6
ISBN-10: 1-946939-87-0

Endorsements

"*Love in Pictures* is a good beach read to put on your summer list. Alexis A. Goring tackles an issue of our times with grace and faith through the characters, using humor and deep emotions to draw in her readers."
–Allison M. Wilson, inspirational writer/editor

"*Love in Pictures* is a beautiful journey of faith, hope, and what it means to take a chance on true love. From quaint cafés in charming, coastal Annapolis to the Mediterranean seashore in Italy, this inspiring tale lifts the heart and soul. I couldn't put it down once I started!" – Jessica Brodie, award-winning Christian journalist, author, and blogger

"With a deft hand, Alexis A. Goring conveys the power and beauty of love in her charming story, *Love in Pictures*. Readers of varied backgrounds and cultures will readily connect with her engaging characters and their search for healing, forgiveness, and acceptance. Goring has written more than a "Will they or won't they?" romance. Her modern love story will touch the hearts of women looking for something more than a happy ending. And they'll find it within the pages of *Love in Pictures*!" – Robin W. Pearson, Contemporary Women's Fiction Author

"*Love in Pictures* is a story for hungry hearts, open hearts, and hearts in need of hope. Alexis has managed to navigate one of our country's most divisive issues in a compassionate and respectful manner, which hopefully will spark future conversations on how we can be the change we seek. So much more than a contemporary romance story, *Love in Pictures* will take readers on a journey to challenge their own long-held perceptions about worthiness and how love can be found and thrive in unexpected places." – Quantrilla Ard, writer at The PhD Mamma

"Alexis A. Goring has a way of telling the sweetest of stories. *Love in Pictures* is no exception." – Cindy Flores Martinez, USA Today bestselling author of sweet and Christian romance

"*Love in Pictures* is a heartfelt and tender book with a happy ending that will take you on the roller coaster ride of love surviving crisis and having the strength to survive. You will feel enchanted as you read this wonderfully written book." – Naeem A. Newman, MD

This book is dedicated to:

True Love. May it always win!

Acknowledgments

First and foremost, I want to thank God. He's my Lord, Savior, Redeemer, and best friend. I am grateful for this writing gift He's given me, and I hope that my words will help win souls to His Son, Jesus Christ.

Quantrilla Ard who brainstormed with me, gave great feedback for the chapters in my story, and helped prevent writer's block from suffocating my creativity. You've been my unofficial writing coach!

Vanessa Riley, my author friend, who encouraged me in my writing journey and reminded me that the best cure for sleepless nights is to write!

Abby Breuklander: Thank you for helping me get unstuck in a few places as I wrote this story. I appreciate your listening to me talk it out when I could not figure out a scene or two then helping me work through it.

Pepper Basham, speech-language pathologist, M.S. CCC-SLP. Thank you for sharing insights from your work as an SLP to help inspire me as I wrote Mrs. Emerson's character.

Cris Carey, speech language pathologist, who checked my story's scenes that contained therapy sessions for accuracy and believability. Thank you!

Dr. Naeem Newman and Dr. Ronda Wells: Thank you for lending your professional expertise to ensure that the hospital scene was true to real life.

Doris E. McMillon, thank you for lending your media industry expertise to help me make Logan's journey to his professional career dreams believable.

Cynthia Hickey, my publisher: Thank you for believing in me and publishing my stories!

Thank you to those who wrote endorsements for my book! I value your thoughts about my characters and storytelling.

Thank you to my church family and pastors. You all are such a kind, genuine, and wonderful support. God bless you!

Thank you to all of my family members, especially my mom and dad who believe in my creative dreams and are willing to help me in my journey.

ALEXIS GORING

Chapter 1

Michelle Hadley stared at the Lightroom editing screen on her computer and studied the newlywed couple she'd captured in the photo.

The bride held a beautiful bouquet of soft blue and pastel pink hydrangeas near her waist, while the handsome groom with skin the color of coffee stood close behind her, holding her in a loving embrace, kissing her forehead.

Michelle sipped her favorite green tea as she sat and worked at Marie's Mocha Café and sighed. The forehead kiss. So romantic. Meant he loved her brains, not just her beauty.

The bride's olive skin glowed, and her dark brown tresses cascaded down her shoulders and rested at her waist. She peered at the flowers she held in her manicured hands, her golden-brown eyes sparkling, a sweet smile tugging at the corner of her lips. Everything about this picture showed that this couple was in love and happy to say I do, not only on their wedding day, but every day they spent together thereafter.

Ah, love. Something she might never experience.

She bit her bottom lip. Would she ever meet a great guy and be blessed with a real-life happily ever after?

She reached for her cup and took a sip to the calming accompaniment of the smoothie machine.

She tapped her fingers on her computer keyboard and opened Facebook Messenger. Writing messages to her best friend, Juliana Fernandes, who worked as a writer for *Bridal Mode Magazine,* also soothed her nerves.

Michelle: *Hey, girl. What's up?*

Juliana: *Michelle, mi amiga, it's been such a long day! Want to meet me for lunch? I could use a little girl talk.*

Michelle: *Sorry. I'm editing photos, and I'm on deadline.*

Juliana: *Oh yes, my lovely friend the wedding photographer who's all work and no play.*

Michelle: *What do you mean?*

Juliana: *You never make time for fun.*

Michelle: *Yeah, I do. I meet up with you, and we go shopping and for coffee.*

Juliana: *Yes, and I love our time together, but girl, you need to meet a man and go out on a date, several dates, with several eligible bachelors. I could find one for you. I meet plenty in my line of work.*

Michelle: *Aren't most of those men you interview getting married?*

Juliana: *Oh yeah, that's right. ☺ But they have*

brothers, cousins and friends! Amiga, I could totally hook you up!

Michelle: *Lol. Thanks, but no thanks. God is my matchmaker.*

Juliana: *Yeah? Well, sometimes God uses good friends like me to pull the strings.*

Michelle: *Sorry to cut this short, but I need to get back to work.*

Juliana: *And then you do that.*

Michelle: *Do what?*

Juliana: *When I get too close to the truth, you end the conversation.*

Michelle: *Jules, you're taking this way too personal.*

Juliana: *You know I'm right. But it's okay, I forgive you! Now go ahead and get back to work. Meanwhile, I'm going to pray that God shows me how to help you meet a great guy, and then I can be your maid of honor in your wedding. Oh my gosh, girl, who do you trust enough to be your wedding photographer? You're such a good photographer. But you cannot photograph your own wedding.*

Michelle chuckled as she typed a reply.

Michelle: *Lol. Let's talk about this when I actually get engaged to Mr. Right.*

Juliana: *Lol. Okay, amiga. Ciao!*

Michelle: *Ciao, girl!*

Michelle smiled as she shut down her Messenger app. Not chatting with friends would make it easier for her to focus on her work. As she edited the photos of her latest wedding, the point Juliana made came to mind. If she was always busy working, she would not have time to meet Mr.

Right.

She shook her head. Why couldn't Mr. Right find her? *Is there a man for me, God?* Did she want one? She loved the freedom of her single life.

She reached for her tea. The cup slipped through her grasp and splattered across the floor near the entrance to the ordering line.

A man came into her view. Before she could open her mouth to issue a warning, he hit the liquid, slipped, and fell.

Michelle jolted to her feet and bent to assist him. She reached for his arm to help him up. "I am so sorry! I don't know how that happened."

The man grasped her by the hand and pulled himself to a standing position with the agility of an athlete. He met her eyes and flashed an award-winning smile. His ocean-blue eyes took her breath away. At his smile, her heart skipped several beats.

He finger-combed his dark-brown hair and laughed. "I didn't plan to take a spill today, but that's okay."

Warmth rose to Michelle's cheeks. If her hazelnut skin were a few shades lighter, she'd be red.

"Besides, if I didn't take that spill, I wouldn't have met you." He winked, and her heart pounded.

She had to get herself together. He was gorgeous, and he winked, but that didn't mean anything special. Plenty of men flirted with women. Completely normal.

But it wasn't something that happened to her.

She hadn't felt giddy like this in years. She forced a smile and laughed nervously. "Oh yes, well…"

The handsome gentleman reached out to shake her hand. "Logan Emerson. I come here for lunch often, but I've never seen you here before. It's a pleasure to meet you."

"I'm Michelle. I edit photos here a lot." She managed to speak in a steady voice.

Logan glanced at her laptop. "At least your computer didn't take a fall."

Michelle gave a genuine laugh. "Tell me about it."

Logan glanced at the line, which was getting shorter by the minute, and then at his watch, before turning his attention back to her. "Hey, I've got to eat and run, but I'd love to have lunch with you here one day. My treat. What do you say?"

"I…uh." She had to get it together. "I'm too busy!"

The light in Logan's eyes dimmed at her blurted confession. He smiled and reached out, touching her arm, an innocent caress. "Well, I'd love to meet you here one day for lunch when you're less busy."

All Michelle could do was nod.

"I've got to go. God bless you."

Was he a Christian, or did he just say God bless you to everyone? As Logan got into line, Michelle returned to her seat. She stopped herself from banging her head on the table. She let a perfect specimen of a man walk away without taking him up on his offer of a lunch date. What was wrong with her? He was interested in her, but she told him she was too busy. Too busy! Juliana was right. She was all work and no fun.

Suddenly, the hum of the smoothie machine sent shivers up her arms. She packed her things, grabbed her purse, and made a quick exit.

~*~

Logan jogged at a steady pace. His sneaker-clad feet pounded the concrete pavement of the trail through Pond Park within a few miles of Marie's Mocha Café in the Bowie shopping center. It was the place where he met the intriguing, too-busy-for-lunch woman with the gorgeous honey-brown eyes and sweet personality. Now he could not get her off his mind.

Footfalls that were far behind Logan became louder and sounded closer. Logan turned to his left just as his best friend Cameron caught up.

"Man. Your speed improves every morning. Are you on steroids?"

Logan chuckled. "No. I just eat healthy and keep up the exercise."

Cameron stopped to catch his breath. He rested his hands on his knees and panted. Meanwhile, Logan ran circles around him. "Come on, Cam. You can do it. We've got two more miles to run before quitting time."

Cameron cast a look at Logan before shaking his head and returning to running. This time, Cameron kept Logan's pace. "So what's going on, man?"

Logan looked at Cameron. "Why do you ask?"

"You seem preoccupied. Like you're thinking too hard."

Logan paused. Should he talk about the girl at the café? "I met a girl."

Cameron shot a quick glance at him and raised his eyebrows. "Really? Where?"

"At Marie's Mocha."

"Cool. When?"

"This morning, before our jog."

"You mean before our run. Seriously, Logan. Can we slow down the pace?"

Logan slowed down by a few paces, and Cameron breathed a sigh of relief. "Okay. Tell me about her."

"She's beautiful. Sweet…and very busy."

Cameron narrowed his eyes.

"She said she was too busy for me to treat her to lunch."

Cameron laughed.

Logan furrowed his brow. "What's so funny?"

Cameron reached out and slapped Logan's upper back. "This is progress. You haven't even looked at another woman since London broke your heart and chose her career over marrying you. This is good. Now it's time to throw her picture away that you keep in your office."

Logan paused. "Yeah. You're right."

Cameron ran in front of Logan and faced him while jogging backwards. "I'm so proud of you, man. What's her name?"

A woman approached Cameron from behind. "Cameron, watch out!"

But it was too late. He crashed into the woman, and they both fell to the ground. Logan rushed to the woman's side and reached down to pick her up. "Hey. I apologize for my friend. He wasn't watching where he was going."

As he helped the woman to her feet, he took a closer look at her. "Michelle?"

Recognition dawned in her eyes. "Logan?"

Cameron, who was standing now, interrupted. "Wait, you two know each other?"

Logan and Michelle didn't look at Cameron but answered in unison. "Yes."

Cameron paused. "How?"

Logan turned to Cameron. "Cameron this is Michelle, the woman that I ran into at the café earlier today. Michelle, this is Cameron. He's my best friend and jogging buddy."

Michelle smiled. She extended her hand. "Nice to meet you, Cameron."

Cameron shook Michelle's hand. "Same."

Michelle withdrew her hand and looked at Logan. "It's nice seeing you again, but I need to go. I was just on my way to meet a client."

Logan nodded. "Understood."

Michelle cast a timid smile before continuing on.

Cameron leaned in and spoke to Logan in a low voice. "Now there's a woman who will make you forget about London. Don't let her slip through your fingers."

Logan slapped Cameron on his shoulders. "Thanks for the advice, man. Let's finish our run." He took off ahead of Cameron, his footfalls a few paces behind. But Logan wasn't slowing down. Running was his release. The faster he ran, the clearer his mind became and the more he could focus and think through things. Right now, he had to think about ways to get Michelle to agree to a lunch date.

Yes, she was busy, but Logan was determined. He was ready to leave London in the past and move forward with his life. He was ready to get back into the dating game. Only he didn't want to play the field. He was interested in one woman.

Michelle.

Chapter 2

Michelle sat in her favorite half booth at her favorite café within earshot of the smoothie machine. People's chatter tended to drown out the machine's noise everywhere else except this cozy area. Today she was writing a blog post for her business website.

The sound of waves crashing against the seashore distracted her from her writing.

Ugh. She picked up her cell phone. She puffed out a breath as she read the text. It was her wanna-be-matchmaker best friend.

Juliana: *If you run into that gorgeous man today, you better say yes to that lunch date.*

Michelle: *Girl, let me work.*

Juliana: *How about, 'Girl, what color do you want your bridesmaid dress to be?'*

Michelle chuckled. Juliana could not be serious. Maybe working at a wedding magazine every weekday had marriage and romance on Juliana's mind, but Michelle was more practical. She never dreamed of her wedding day as a little girl, and as an adult who had a lot of disappointments in dating, she'd probably never find her happily ever after. But being a wedding photographer and working with such lovely couples kept the hope in her heart alive that maybe one day it would be her in the designer wedding dress, walking down the aisle to a future of bliss with the one man she could not live without.

Juliana: *Hello? Earth to Michelle.*

Michelle blinked. The sound of the text message alert broke her out of her daydream. Her eyes focused on her half-finished blog post. She turned back to her cell phone.

Michelle: *Sorry, girl. Got to go.*

Juliana: *Sigh. I will pray that you get a life.*

Michelle: *Go back to work, girl. Talk to you later!*

She powered off her cell phone to avoid future interruptions. Just as she returned to typing, something else distracted her. Only this time, the interruption was about 5'8", donned in athletic clothes, and towered over her. Michelle looked up into Logan's sea-blue eyes. Juliana's text message returned to Michelle's mind, and heat rose from her neck to her cheeks. The man smiled, arresting Michelle's attention with his pearly whites. He should be a TV journalist. Ladies everywhere would watch the news every day just to see him.

"Hey." His rich, tenor voice resonated like an Irish Andrea Bocelli.

"Hey."

"It's good to see you again."

"You too."

The man extended his right hand. "I'm Logan. Remember me?"

Michelle paused, willing her heart to be still. "Yes."

She didn't shake his hand. He looked embarrassed and withdrew his. He glanced at the two people in line then returned his gaze to Michelle. "Did you eat yet? How about I treat you to lunch?"

Michelle's heart fluttered. She paused again. Logan raised an eyebrow.

"I'm sorry, Logan. I'm working."

"Aw, come on, even working girls got to eat."

Michelle chuckled. Maybe it wasn't a bad idea. He was really cute. And nice. "Sure. You can join me for lunch, but I can buy my own food."

Logan shrugged. "Okay."

Michelle picked up her purse, stood, and followed Logan to the ordering counter. He placed his order and paid for it. But when Michelle tried to pay for hers, the cashier paused and looked at Michelle with apologetic eyes. "I'm sorry, ma'am, but your card was declined."

Michelle's cheeks warmed. Before she could reach in her purse for another card, Logan stepped in. He flashed her an easy smile and paid for her meal in cash.

Too embarrassed to speak, Michelle slipped her card back into her wallet and gripped her purse as she followed Logan to the pickup line.

"So, Michelle, are you always here on Sundays? I thought for sure that you'd be here only during the weekdays."

"Yes. I'm here just about every day or night."

Logan raised both of his eyebrows. "Is this your office?"

"You could say that."

The server placed their orders on the counter. Michelle reached for her French toast bagel with honey walnut cream cheese, and Logan grabbed his order of a grilled cheese sandwich with a half bowl of tomato soup. Together, they walked to the nearest booth.

Logan allowed Michelle to settle in, then he placed his food on the table and sat in in the chair across from her. "So, what are you working on today?"

"A blog post."

Logan bit into his sandwich. "Cool. About what?"

"I'm looking for models for a photo shoot I'm staging."

Logan nodded as he took another bite of his sandwich and swallowed. "What's that like?"

"I'm trying to train aspiring photographers how to shoot a couple's engagement session."

Logan nodded and took another big bite of his sandwich, which was half gone.

"Who are the couples?"

Michelle paused. She poked at her untouched bagel.

Logan chuckled. "You should eat. We can talk when you're done."

His words warmed her heart. It wasn't every day that a guy spending time with her just about read her mind. She smiled. "Thanks." She reached for her bagel and spread the cream cheese on it. She bit into it and closed her eyes, savoring the perfect medley of flavors.

It wasn't until she'd consumed the entire bagel that she locked eyes with Logan and her cheeks warmed. He'd been staring at her, and his eyes twinkled like stars in the midnight sky. A smile tugged at the corner of his lips. Was he laughing at her?

Logan pointed to the corner of her lips. "You, you have something there."

She had food on her mouth while eating in front of him? If only the tiled floor would open up and swallow her whole.

She grabbed a napkin and wiped her full mouth. She gazed at him for approval. Logan chuckled, picked up a clean paper napkin, and reached across the table. He wiped the upper left side of her mouth, just above her lips. Lips that she was suddenly grateful were coated in pink lipstick today, the kind that lasts twenty-four hours. His touch was gentle and swift. Her heart fluttered.

Logan withdrew the napkin and crumbled it. "There."

"Thanks."

"Tell me more about this photo shoot."

Michelle noted that she was not the only one with a clean plate. She focused on Logan.

"I'm meeting aspiring photographers on location to teach them how to pose couples and take their pictures outdoors using natural light."

"How do you find couples?"

"Everywhere. I'm a talent scout. I'll walk up to people who look like models, introduce myself, tell them what I'm doing, and see if they agree. I also draw from my pool of clients."

"Do you do headshot sessions too?"

"Yes. Why?"

"I'm looking for a photographer to take some for my professional social media. Do you think I'm photogenic?" He tilted his head.

Michelle chuckled.

"So, can we set this up?"

Michelle sipped her water. "What?"

"You know, set up a shoot. I'd like for you to be my photographer. That is, if you're not too busy."

Her heart said "yes" to working with him but her head and all of her insecurities said "no". "I, uh...I..."

He reached in his pocket, retrieved his business card, and handed it to her. "Think about it, and when you're ready, call me." He glanced at his watch, stood, and stacked Michelle's empty tray on top of his. "I've got to run—literally. But I hope to see you again, sometime soon."

"Me too," she squeaked.

Logan picked up the trays and headed in the direction of the trash bins.

Michelle leaned on the table, rubbed her temples, and cast her gaze heavenward. *Dear God, what am I getting myself into? Please don't let me mess this up.*

Her gaze rested on the business card, and she picked it up. Hmm, he worked for a newspaper. She could always call him to take him up on his offer. After all, she was more experienced with doing headshots than she was with dating. This would be an easy job and a great way to get to know him better.

She brushed her thoughts about Logan aside and pulled her laptop closer. She needed to finish the blog post. Calling Logan would happen later.

Maybe.

Chapter 3

Michelle worked out to her favorite Pilates video in the comfort of her parents' home. She drank in the peace and solitude like her favorite pineapple smoothie. Living with her parents allowed her to save money toward her own place, but she craved these moments alone.

Just as she finished her workout and completed her cool-down routine of full body stretches, the blare of the house alarm interrupted her peace.

Her pulse quickened.

Her brother, Marcel, walked into the family room. Michelle huffed and glared at her older brother. "You scared me! Did you forget the code?"

He gave a sheepish shrug.

She rushed to the nearby laundry room and punched in the code then breathed a sigh of relief as quiet returned to the house. As she returned to the family room, she shook her head at him.

"What? Just because I got married and moved out doesn't mean I can't visit, right?"

Michelle folded her arms and quirked an eyebrow. "Right."

Marcel tossed his keys on to the kitchen counter and opened the refrigerator. "When are you moving out?"

Michelle rubbed her temples. Her work out was over, but she was not in a conversational mood. She turned off the TV. "When I get the money to afford my own place."

Marcel raised an eyebrow. "You creative types never have money. You should have become a doctor like me." He took a swig of the orange juice straight from the bottle.

Michelle's eyes widened. "Does your wife allow you to do that?"

He set the bottle down and opened his hands. "What? It's almost empty."

Michelle tsked. She came and sat on a kitchen stool. "Some things never change."

Marcel harrumphed. "Yeah, like my pretty sister who at the age of twenty-nine is still single and living at home."

She narrowed her eyes. "That's mean."

"It's the truth." Marcel glanced at her open notebook computer on the kitchen table. He sat in the chair in front of it and scrolled through.

Logan's LinkedIn profile. Michelle gasped and rushed to Marcel's side. No need for him to see that she was internet stalking Logan. "Nosy, aren't we?"

She reached to close her computer, but Marcel stopped her. "Who's he?"

Heat rose to her cheeks. "Nobody."

He picked up the business card on the kitchen

table next to Michelle's computer. He read it then smirked. "A nobody whose business card just happens to be here too?"

Michelle pulled at her ponytail. She avoided Marcel's intense stare.

"Yes. I mean no. I mean, it's none of your business." She slammed her computer shut, swiped it from Marcel, clutched it to her chest, and stared at her brother. He glared at her as if she had done something wrong.

"Are you dating him?"

"Dating?"

"Yes, sis. Are you dating that white guy?"

Michelle steeled. "That's none of your business."

Marcel rose out of his chair. "As your brother, I'd say it is my business. What did I tell you about those guys? They're no good for you."

Michelle raised her chin. "Why not?"

"History, Michelle. You know what those white slave masters did to the black female slaves. After all they put us through, you are dating one of them?"

Michelle's lower lip quivered. "It's time for you to leave." Her voice was barely a whisper.

Marcel shook his head. "Yeah." He grabbed his keys and paused, looking at Michelle. "Don't do it, sis. It's not worth it."

He grabbed some food from the refrigerator, stuffed it into the grocery bag he'd brought with him, and walked to the front door. Michelle didn't move until she heard him exit the house, then she went to the door. Her hands shook and she fought back tears as she punched in the code to turn the alarm on. If her own brother thought this way, what would strangers think? It was a level of hatred and ignorance that she was not ready to face.

She returned to the kitchen and set her computer on the table. She stared at Logan's business card. She reached for it, tempted to tear it up, but then stopped. Logan was nice. He didn't mean any harm. Maybe she would do the photo shoot for him and then cut off all communication. After all, he'd paid for her lunch. She owed him a favor.

Didn't she?

Chapter 4

Michelle tapped the letters on her cellphone. Her hands shook so much, she dropped her phone twice. She reached for a tissue and rubbed her phone gently. She was lucky that it didn't break and was still working. Thank God for protective covers.

She glanced around her studio. No one else was here to witness her fall apart. She took a deep breath. *Calm down girl. It's just a photo shoot. You've done hundreds of these since starting your photography business. You've got this.*

Michelle put her phone down on her workstation desk and rubbed her throbbing temple. It wasn't every day that she agreed to photograph a client who expressed interest in dating her. Correction. She never mixed business with pleasure, so this was the first and probably the last time she'd allow her heart to make a decision that could affect her work. Heat rose to her face. She would do the headshot photo shoot and play this by ear. Even if she decided not to date Logan, they could be friends.

The text alert sound jolted her out of her thoughts and turned her attention to her workstation. She picked up the phone and sighed. Juliana. Thank God. She could calm her down.

Juliana: *What's good, amiga?*

Michelle: *Pray for me.*

Juliana: *Why?*

Michelle: *Just pray.*

Juliana: *Oh, is this about that guy from the café? Are you two going on a date?*

Michelle: *Not really. More like a photo shoot.*

Juliana sent an excited emoji. *How fun! Where?*

Michelle: *My studio.*

Juliana: *Amiga, I know just how to help you.*

Michelle: *Please do.*

After a minute of silence from Juliana, Michelle glanced at her watch. Juliana never took more than five seconds to write a reply. She frowned.

Michelle: *Jules?*

Juliana: *I've got you, amiga. Sorry. Tied up at work. We'll chat soon! Prayers up!*

Michelle closed her eyes, inhaled a deep breath, and slowly let it out. She sent up a silent prayer of her own. It was just a photo shoot, a professional headshot session that only took fifteen minutes. This was not a big deal. It was not a date. She turned her attention to adjusting the lighting in her studio and glanced at the clock on her wall. Five minutes to noon. Logan would be here soon.

~*~

Logan enjoyed the beautiful, bright, sunny day and the salty scent of fresh bay water in the air as he strolled from the parking lot to the studio like a man going on a GQ photo shoot. This session with Michelle could be the start of a beautiful friendship and hopefully something more as he geared up the nerve to ask her out.

So far, the location and exterior decoration impressed him. The place was in the heart of Annapolis. A coffee shop and a bookstore sandwiched her studio. Above the door was a canary-yellow sign with pink, bold letters that announced Love in Pictures.

Logan reached for the knob and opened the door. The subtle scent of vanilla wafted to his nose. The studio itself was clean, orderly, professional looking, and had a very feminine touch in its décor.

He stood at the receptionist desk but saw no one. Neither could he locate a bell, a speakerphone, anything to let Michelle know he was here. Just as he turned to search for a doorbell, a few words stilled him.

"Good afternoon, Logan."

The soft and familiar sound of Michelle's voice soothed his nerves. He turned to face her and smiled. A pink skirt, yellow top, and yellow heels set off her raven-black hair that framed her face and fell to her shoulders. He cleared his throat. "Good afternoon."

She curved her rose-pink painted lips upward in a sweet smile. "Are you ready for your session?"

"I was born ready."

Michelle giggled. "I bet you were." She stepped aside and gestured to him. "Follow me."

He obeyed orders, walking behind her as she led

him through the lobby, down the corridor, and into a room with various pieces of lighting equipment. He only recognized the incandescent lights from the popular news studio he visited in downtown Washington, D.C.

"I'll take your jacket."

Michelle's words knocked him out of his train of thought. He took off his suitcoat and handed it to her.

"Have a seat here, please. I need to do your makeup."

Logan raised his eyebrows.

She laughed. "I'm only applying foundation to keep your skin looking even and flawless under the lighting."

Logan sat and tapped his right foot on the floor.

That familiar blush rose to Michelle's hazelnut-toned face again. He caught a glimpse of her smile as she turned away. When she turned back, she was all business.

He cleared his throat as he mustered the courage to carry on a normal conversation. "Do you do makeup for all of your clients?"

"Mainly just for the guys who want headshots. The ladies usually come with theirs already done."

"Ah, I see."

She stepped back and studied Logan's face as if she was determining whether her work was finished. She nodded and put the compact and brush away. "All done." She handed him a mirror.

He peered at his reflection and was impressed by her work. She'd even managed to conceal a pimple below his chin. This lady was a pro.

"Shall we?"

He rose and followed her across the room to a black stool in front of what looked like a green screen but had a black curtain as the backdrop. She turned on the lights and adjusted it for the perfect glow.

"Sit down, please."

He seated himself and swiveled until he faced Michelle, who had stepped behind what looked like a DSLR camera positioned on a tripod.

"We're going to take a few photos with you sitting, and we'll take the rest with you standing with your back to the black curtain."

Michelle held up three fingers. "Starting on the count of three. Smile for me."

Logan flashed his best grin, glad that he just went to the dentist this morning.

The photo shoot progressed like clockwork, and before Logan knew it, they were done. Michelle stepped from behind her camera. "Great work. You're a natural."

"I could say the same about you." He tapped his foot and cleared his throat. She scrunched her forehead. Well, it was now or never. "Hey, w-w-w-would."

His face heated. His nerves had triggered his stuttering. He'd hoped to hide his speech impediment from her, but it always showed up in situations like these. It was the number one reason why the producers at that station in D.C. wouldn't hire him as on-air talent.

He gazed to the ground. He never should have come. When he mustered up the courage to resume eye contact, he found Michelle studying him, her eyes and face soft.

She touched his arm. "Everything okay?"

Logan nodded. "Y-y-yes." He glanced at his watch on his left wrist, trying to buy time to regain control over his speech. Her touch was soft and gentle. It was like she wanted to help him and be there for him. But now was not the time to talk. He sidestepped and willed his words to flow. "I've got to go. Thanks for the photo shoot."

Michelle broke contact with him. "Okay, thanks for being my client."

Logan finger-combed his hair and glanced around. Where was the exit?

"Follow me. I'll show you the way out."

Five minutes later, Logan sat in his car and hit his steering wheel. Why did his stuttering show up at the most inconvenient times? It kept him from getting a job at the TV station, and it was keeping him from asking out Michelle.

He reached for his phone to call his mom, a successful speech therapist who had helped many clients overcome their stuttering. Unfortunately, her best efforts had helped but not healed Logan's problem. But she did have techniques that assisted him when his stuttering flared. The phone rang then went to voicemail.

"H-h-hey Mom. Can I come over? I need your help."

After leaving a message, he rested his phone on the passenger seat of his car and gazed at the studio's front door. Michelle was so sweet. She wanted to help him, he could tell. But how did he open up to her about this problem? Logan shifted into drive and pulled away. *God, help me.*

Chapter 5

Michelle sat across the table from Juliana at their favorite coffee shop and sipped her ice water. "I can't believe you drink that stuff."

Juliana only grinned and sipped her caramel macchiato for a few more moments before placing her cup on the table and staring at Michelle. "Spill it."

She sank deeper into her chair. Should she tell Juliana? She would be more understanding than most. "He stutters."

Juliana's hazel eyes filled with tears. "Oh, Michelle. Logan stutters?"

She nodded.

Juliana reached across the table and held Michelle by the hands. "I know that must bring back a lot of sad memories."

Michelle sighed. She withdrew from Juliana's comforting touch and rubbed the sides of her head. As a young child, her cousin Malcolm's school peers bullied him for his constant stuttering, and it hurt him deeply. It hurt him so much that he took his life. She shuddered as she remembered her aunt and uncle's faces at their son's funeral. Grief personified. He was only twelve. He hadn't even really lived life, and due to those relentless taunts from those cruel bullies, he was dead.

Fire rose within her. She hated injustice in every form, especially when it affected a loved one. "He didn't have to die. Kids can be so cruel." Michelle fiddled with the straw in her tall, half-empty glass of water.

Juliana sipped her coffee. "Yeah, kids can be cruel, but Logan is a survivor. He didn't let his stuttering stop him from living. Thank God. He found a way to cope and moved on. Think about it, Miche. He never would have met you."

Michelle shrugged. "Yeah, I guess that's a good thing."

"And so is your empathy. He needs a friend who understands. Maybe this could draw you two closer."

Michelle wiped a tear from her eye, reached for a napkin, and used it as a tissue. Juliana sat by, sipping her coffee as Michelle straightened the hem of her silk blouse and smoothed her hair. She then wrapped her hands around her half-full cup of ice water. "Maybe you're right."

Juliana put her cup down and leaned in. "Amiga, of course I'm right. God brought this man into your life for a reason. I have great expectations for this relationship."

A half laugh escaped Michelle. "We're not in a relationship."

Juliana raised an eyebrow. "Yet." She smirked before glancing at her watch. "Alright, amiga. I need to get back to work before they fire me for being a few minutes late."

Juliana was like the sister she never had. "Thanks, girl. I needed this talk."

At the ringing of her phone, Juliana reached into her purse and stood. "Of course. That's what friends are for. I've got to go and take this call. Later, amiga!" She blew air kisses before answering her phone and rushing out the door.

Michelle removed the straw from her glass and gulped down the remainder of its ice-cold water. The coolness refreshed her. She pulled out her phone and checked her calendar. What was Logan doing today? Was he okay? They hadn't spoken since he left the photo shoot. She had his number from his business card. Maybe she should text him?

After sending up a prayer, she tapped the digital keyboard. She'd let him know she was thinking about him as a friend. Nothing flirty. Just a platonic message, reaching out to show she cared.

~*~

As Logan found a parking space near his mom's private practice, a familiar, lighthearted jingle let him know he had a text message. He reached for his phone. He only had a minute to spare before his appointment with his mother.

Oh, it was from Michelle. She asked how he was doing after the photo shoot. Very sweet and business-like. She said she would send a link to her online gallery of his headshots by tomorrow and that he would receive a CD containing the headshots in the mail by next week unless he wanted to meet her in person to pick it up.

Hmm, she left it open for them to meet in person. He wanted to see her again, but he didn't want to embarrass himself by stuttering in her presence. He'd probably have to explain his disability the next time he saw her. But at the same time, he wanted to see her. Picking up the CD of his headshots would be the perfect excuse to gaze into her honey-brown eyes.

Mom was expecting him. Michelle's text would have to wait. He hustled inside where both a blast of cold air and the receptionist greeted him.

"Hey, Sara. I'm here to see my mom."

The petite receptionist with fire-red hair and shamrock-green eyes looked up. "Hey, Logan. Go back to her office. She's waiting for you."

He gulped. His mom valued promptness. "Thanks."

Sara nodded before returning her attention to the paperwork on her desk. He sauntered down the short hallway and turned the corner to face his mother's closed office door. He paused before knocking.

"Who is it?" His mother's voice was melodious and pitch-perfect. She was the reason Logan was able to manage his stuttering.

He broke free of his inner thoughts and opened the door. "H-h-hey." He paused. "Hey, Mom."

Mom came around her desk and engulfed him in a hug. "Hey, honey."

Logan hugged her back. She pulled away. Logan shut her door then sank into the couch.

"We have an hour to work together. I take it your stuttering is resurfacing?"

Logan nodded.

"When did this happen, and what were you doing when it happened?"

Thoughts of Michelle filled his mind and heat rose to his face.

"It happened at a ph-ph-ph-photoshoot on Monday."

Mom nodded. "Let's do our fluency-shaping exercises."

He placed his right hand over his voice box and recited his vowels.

He practiced the easy onset technique Mom taught him as she monitored his airflow and speech. He spent the hour with her, following her instructions as she guided him through their tried-and-true exercises.

After their time was up, his confidence returned. Next time he met Michelle, he wouldn't stutter. "Thanks, Mom."

"You're welcome, honey. Now tell me about her."

Logan raised his eyebrows. "Who?"

Mom tilted her head. "The girl that made you stutter."

"I didn't say it was a girl."

"You didn't have to. I know."

He laughed. Whenever he had a crush on a girl and tried to talk to her, he would stutter. He thought he'd outgrown that flaw until he met Michelle.

Mom glanced at the clock. "You can tell me about her later. My next client should be here in a few minutes."

He stood. "Thanks for helping."

"Anytime, darling. I'm always here for you."

Not until he settled into the driver seat of his car did he realize that he never replied to Michelle's text. He retrieved his phone and typed a response. "Let's meet tomorrow. At our place."

Now, if he could just keep from stuttering.

Chapter 6

Logan strolled into Marie's Mocha Café humming to himself, practicing vocal exercises to the tune of a Michael Bublé song as he waited for Michelle to arrive for lunch. He glanced at his watch as he slid into an empty booth and peered around. She should be here with his photo CD any minute.

He turned his humming into soft singing. He was so engrossed in the tune he didn't realize someone was listening until Michelle slid into the empty seat across from him.

He held back a whistle. Today she wore a blue skirt that hugged her curves, a fancy white top that bared her toned shoulders and played off her flawless hazelnut skin. Wow, she was gorgeous.

Michelle placed her purse on the booth seat and leaned in with a little smile on her face. "Hey there. I didn't know you could sing."

Logan chuckled. "Yeah, well, I'm not that great. My mom is a professionally trained singer."

Michelle's eyes widened. "Really?"

"She changed career paths when she realized she wasn't going to be the next Joni Mitchell."

"What does she do now?"

"She became a speech language pathologist, and she's pretty good. Pretty famous here in Maryland. She helps me with my stuttering."

Michelle's golden-brown eyes glowed with compassion.

"I'm sure you noticed that last time we spoke."

She nodded, and her hands trembled. Her eyes glistened. Was something wrong? He reached out to squeeze her hands. Whatever the problem was, he wanted to fix it. "What's the matter?"

"My cousin Malcolm used to stutter."

"Really? How is he doing now?"

A tear streaked down her cheek. "We lost him."

Logan drew back. "What?"

She wrung her hands as she spoke. "His peers in school bullied him relentlessly. He didn't tell his parents. They found out after the funeral. If we had known what he was going through when he was alive, we would have told him he was wonderful the way he was, that we couldn't live without him, and suicide wasn't the answer. Malcolm was a gift to everyone. He didn't deserve to think he was unloved." She covered her face.

Logan slipped out of his seat, slid next to her, held her close, and let her cry. She soaked his shirt with her tears. *Dear Lord, please help me to help her. Show me how.*

A few minutes later, she wiped the tears from her face and pushed away. "I'm sorry."

He touched her chin and turned her face toward

his. "Don't be sorry. You can tell me anything."

Michelle stifled a laugh. "You sound like a therapist."

Logan chuckled.

"Thanks."

Well, now was better than ever. He'd better ask her out before another man swooped in and swept her off her feet. He cleared his throat and prayed that he would not stutter. "Would you like to go out with me sometime? Somewhere other than here?"

She nodded. "Where would you like to meet?"

"You can meet me on my boat. That's where I live."

Michelle's jaw dropped. "You have a yacht?"

"Yes, in Annapolis. Not too far from your studio. I'd like to take you sailing across the bay someday too." Logan reached for his cell phone. He tapped the screen, pulled up an exterior photo of his boat, and sent it to her. "Take a look."

She stared at the screen with her mouth agape. "Wow, it's gorgeous." She peered at him and tilted her head. "You've got very alluring ideas for dates."

"You haven't seen anything yet."

"Can't wait."

Neither could he. He just hoped he wouldn't blow it.

Chapter 7

Michelle tugged at her snug top and pale-blue skinny jeans as she strolled down the dock to the boat Logan had described. She hoped that she wasn't overdressed—or underdressed. A cool breeze blew through her hair, and the fresh scent of the bay refreshed her soul on this sunny, early summer day.

Though she'd lived here all her life, this was her first time in the marina. She'd never met someone who lived on the water. This was a new experience.

She stopped when she reached a boat that resembled the one in the picture Logan texted her yesterday. It was more gorgeous and expansive in real time. Clearly this was more than a boat. Not knowing much about yachts, Michelle lacked better words to describe this sleek, smooth creation painted in white with blue and gold trimmings. As she reached out to touch it, Logan emerged from the lower deck.

He waved. "Hey there."

"Hey." She smoothed the cool fabric of her comfortable boat-neck top, hoping it wasn't too much. "I didn't know what to wear. This is my first date on a boat."

He gazed at her with his beautiful sea-blue eyes then encircled her waist and drew her in for a hug. "Don't worry. You look beautiful."

Michelle's heart somersaulted. He steadied her in his embrace. "You okay?"

Michelle gathered her wits and focused her attention on the horizon. "Does she have a name?"

Logan chuckled. "Yes, she does. Her legal name is Talaria 48. She's a Hinckley."

"Hinckley?"

"Yes. Only the best boat maker and yacht experience in America." He stepped ahead of Michelle on the slip then turned and reached for her. "Come aboard, my lady."

Michelle's neck warmed. She placed her hand in his and stepped onto the swaying boat.

She allowed him to continue holding her hand until they settled into the cockpit where he had prepared a light dinner. The aroma of apricot-glazed baked chicken mixed with the scent of fresh salad drizzled with lemon vinaigrette and sweet sparkling apple cider. By the looks of it, he was a very talented chef.

He moved so that Michelle could take a seat then settled across the table. He reached out and took Michelle's hands into his. "I'd like to pray, if that's okay."

Michelle's heart warmed. He was a man of faith in God too? In a world where it looked like most men threw chivalry out the window, Logan was slowly but surely becoming her knight in shining armor. Not that she believed in fairy tales and happily ever after romances. Logan cleared his throat, jolting Michelle out of her thoughts. "Sorry. I'd love for you pray for our food."

Logan bowed his head while Michelle closed her eyes.

"Dear God, thank you for this perfect weather and for Michelle's friendship. Please bless our first date together. May the food strengthen and nourish our bodies. In Jesus' name I pray, Amen."

She wanted to know more about Logan. She hoped this was the first of many dates and shared adventures. That is, if Marcel didn't ruin her budding romance.

"Ready to eat?"

"You've really outdone yourself. This is a treat."

"Thanks."

They unfolded their napkins and tucked the fine cream-colored cloth in their laps. He sipped water from a crystal glass, and her fork clinked against the plate as she scooped up a piece of chicken. They chatted throughout the meal.

All too soon it was over, and Logan stood to clear the dishes. "Would you like to watch the sunset together before you drive home?"

"I'd love to."

"Great. I hope you brought your camera."

"Always."

She followed him to the deck just as the sun touched the western horizon over the city. The colors of pink, deep orange, and yellow blended with the sky's beautiful navy blue. She slipped her phone from her purse and clicked pictures of the sunset.

Logan grabbed her by the arm. "Let's take a picture together."

She settled back in her seat, cuddled close to him, and held her camera out as far as her arm could stretch. "Ready?"

He nodded.

She leaned in so they were barely cheek-to-cheek then pressed the button to flip the camera to take selfies. "Smile!"

He grinned, and her hands shook at the sight of his pearly whites.

He reached for the camera. "Allow me." He pressed the button, and the camera made a quiet shutter noise as it snapped their photo. He handed the camera back to her.

"It's perfect."

"You're perfect."

"Aw, you're sweet."

"Send it to me."

When she gazed up from her phone, Logan watched her with a twinkle in his eyes. "What?"

"You're adorable."

"Thanks for the dinner, Logan. It was delicious. And your home is amazing."

"Home, sweet home."

Her phone chimed a text alert that reminded her to call Juliana about a photo for the magazine. Wow, it was after nine. Juliana was a morning bird, so she was probably on her way to bed. She shrugged. "I'd better go. Business calls."

"Even now?"

"That's the life of a business owner."

"Oh."

Didn't he understand?

"I'll walk you to your car."

She leaned in and pecked his cheek. "I enjoyed tonight. Until next time."

"Until then."

But would there be one? Maybe Juliana was right. Maybe she was too caught up in her business to catch a good man.

Chapter 8

Michelle picked up her phone and dialed Juliana's work number. She was hoping to catch her in the office. The phone rang twice then on the third ring, Juliana's high-pitched voice answered. "Amiga!"

"Hey, girl. You called me last night. What's up?"

"Oh my goodness, I totally forgot. Logan asked you on a date. That wasn't last night, was it?"

Michelle giggled.

"It was. Tell me all about it."

"It was lovely. He made dinner for me on his yacht."

"He has a yacht? I'm in love. I mean, uh, you should be in love." Michelle laughed so hard her stomach hurt. "It's too early to be in love, Jules."

"It's never too early to be in love when you meet Mr. Right." Juliana was forever the hopeless romantic.

"So, what did you call me about?"

"Oh yes, that. Well, I wanted to ask you if you

would send me a link to your top two favorite wedding day photography galleries from your clients. My editor Brenda is looking for new faces for our website."

Michelle's heartbeat accelerated. She'd been waiting for an opportunity like this to show the world a more diverse face of beauty. Juliana was an editorial assistant for Brenda Worthington, the editor-in-chief of *Bridal Mode Magazine*. Ever since Juliana got the job a few years ago, Michelle had been asking if there was a way to get her very diverse clients on the cover of the magazine.

"It's not the magazine cover, but it's a start, right?"

Juliana's words jolted Michelle out of her thoughts. "Totally. Thanks so much. Let me send you those galleries now."

"Love you. Got to go."

"Love you too, friend. Have a great day." Michelle picked up her laptop, sat on the sofa, and curled her feet beneath her body to think. She logged into her website and scrolled through her favorite galleries. It would be so challenging to choose just two sets of clients and their wedding photos, because she loved them all.

Michelle opened the gallery for Lila and Liam. They were such a lovely couple. Lila was biracial. Liam was British. He had sandy-blond hair and piercing gray eyes. She had curly brown hair, a naturally deep tan, and green eyes that told a story. They deserved to have their faces featured on a bridal magazine's online presence. Just as Michelle sent Lila and Liam's gallery to Juliana, her phone rang again. Still focused, she assumed it was Juliana. "You got the photos?"

"Yeah, I got the photo all right."

Michelle froze. Marcel. And judging by the tone of his voice, he was not in a good mood. What happened? "Hey, Marcel. How are you?"

"How are you?"

She racked her brain to figure out why he sounded mad. Nothing. They hadn't spoken for a few weeks. And she definitely hadn't told him about her date with Logan. "I'm good."

"Yeah, you're real good cozying up with that white boy, aren't you?"

Michelle's blood boiled. She loved her brother but disliked his attitude and his nosiness. "My personal life is my business."

"Not when you put it on Facebook."

Her fingers flew across the keyboard and froze as she gazed at her latest status update. It was a picture of her with Logan, the one they took after dinner on his boat, an innocent pose. She'd texted the photo to him when she'd returned home.

Michelle steeled. "I am living my life and building my career."

"With that white boy?"

"First of all, he's not a boy. He's a grown man, and his name is Logan."

"You're playing with fire. I don't want you to get burned."

She gripped her phone so hard her pulse pounded in her wrist. "Did you need something?"

"Yes. I need my sister to be more careful about who she chooses to date. Don't you remember the incident?"

Michelle's stomach turned. Of course she remembered. How could she not? But Marcel shouldn't judge Logan without knowing him. However, given the severity of the incident and everything related to it, she understood why her brother was wary of white people. "Everyone deserves to be judged by the content of their character, not their skin color."

"Do you think that line of thinking works with the way people of color are oppressed in society? We're judged by our skin color more often than you think."

Michelle grimaced. Why did Marcel have to remind her? Why couldn't everybody just show brotherly love to each other? And why couldn't Marcel face the fact that she liked Logan?

"I have to go now." And for the first time in years, she ended the phone call before her brother had the time to respond.

She tried her best to dismiss her brother's words and the mental residue of his harsh attitude. But she couldn't. His words were stuck on replay. Was she really making a bad choice in dating Logan? He was a good man. She knew this for a fact, and she wanted to get to know him better. She hoped in time, she'd prove her brother wrong.

~*~

Logan hummed to himself, practicing his vocal exercises as he waited in the lobby of ABC 7 News in Arlington, Virginia. Today was the day that could change his career and put him on the path to a job as an on-air reporter. As soon as he confirmed his identity and appointment with the news director, they ushered him into the lobby to wait for Carter Wright.

Just as Logan started tapping his feet, a tall, broad man entered the lobby. "Logan Emerson?"

Logan stood and cast a courteous smile. "I am he."

Carter stepped closer and extended his right hand. "Carter Wright, news director. Nice to meet you."

Logan shook Carter's hand. He prayed to God to help him to not stutter. "Nice to meet you too."

Carter nodded. "Follow me."

Logan followed Carter into the hallway behind the receptionist's desk and to the elevator. Carter pressed the button that to would take them to the tenth floor. After complete silence on the ride up, they stepped off, and Carter opened double glass doors. They meandered by a few cubicles where reporters had their noses buried in notes and their eyes focused on the computers. They stopped in front of another glass door that opened into a spacious office cozied with a conference table, plush blue-fabric chairs, a wide window with an amazing view of the city, and a desk with a black-leather rolling chair.

"Welcome to my office. Have a seat."

Logan settled into the seat across from Carter's desk. Carter settled behind the desk, folded his hands, and leaned back in his chair. He studied Logan. For a moment, Logan swallowed the stuttering that rose in his throat.

"Why do you want to work for me?"

Logan cleared his throat. "I'd like to impact audiences by delivering news that's engaging, relative, and helpful to their welfare."

Carter nodded. "Did you bring your résumé?"

Logan reached into the black folder he'd carried with him, retrieved his résumé, and handed it to Carter. "Yes, sir."

Carter studied it in silence. Finally, after what felt like eons to Logan, Carter regained eye contact with Logan. "So, you're a print journalist."

"Yes, sir."

"And you've won awards for your news and feature stories."

"Yes, sir."

"Why do you want to work in television? You seem to be doing well in print."

"I…I…um."

Heat rose to Logan's face. He couldn't read Carter. *Not now, God.*

"I…w-w-want to be on television because I w-w-want to reach a broader audience." Logan straightened his shoulders. "I may s-s-struggle with my speech, but I can assure you, I will be the most passionate, d-d-dedicated, professional, and effective on-air talent that you've had if you'd only g-g-give me a chance."

Logan imagined the wheels turning in Carter's head. He only hoped that it was turning in his favor.

"Well, I must admit I'm impressed by your go-getter attitude, and your demo reel was flawless. But I'm not sure we can work with you."

Logan's heart dropped to his stomach.

Carter reached into his desk drawer and retrieved a business card. He extended it to Logan. "Sally Bridges is the voice coach for our on-air talent. Call her and tell her I sent you to work with her for four weeks. Then get in touch with me, and we'll do another interview. I'll know then whether or not we can hire you."

Logan received the business card and studied it for a moment. "With all due respect, sir, my mom is a speech language pathologist, and she's been working with me off the books since I was a child. What can this woman do for me in four weeks that my mom couldn't?"

Carter leaned back in his chair. A smile tugged at the corner of his lips. "Let's give it four weeks and see."

Logan did not know if Carter was trying to add humor to this situation or if he was serious. "Really?"

Carter nodded.

Logan gave an inward sigh. This had to work. If it didn't, he may give up on his broadcast journalist dreams. Logan extended his hand. "Thank you for meeting with me today."

Carter shook it. "My pleasure. I'll walk you out."

Logan did his best to maintain his composure as he followed Carter out of his office and onto the elevator. Inside, he was jumping for joy because this was the closest he'd come to being employed by a major TV network. It would be a dream come true.

He'd applied for TV jobs with CBS, CNN, and

other news stations located in the greater D.C. area. Each major news network turned him down, despite his flawless demo reel.

Would Carter be the next employer to reject him?

Chapter 9

Juliana pulled into the public parking lot in downtown Annapolis. The rejuvenating smell of water greeted her whenever she drove near the marina. A cool breeze whipped through her medium-brown hair. The picturesque scenery drew her in, from the pretty blue waterscape and fancy boats in the docks to the quaint shops and the aroma of good food cooking in the many upscale restaurants.

A lighthearted giggle escaped, and she covered her mouth to suppress a delighted squeal as she tried to contain her anticipation. She loved surprises, especially when she was the one behind it. She had the day off from work and knew Michelle was working on a deadline and probably not eating well. Juliana was going to surprise her with brunch from her favorite bistro in downtown Annapolis.

She walked into Sofi's Crepes and ordered her favorites: the veggie crepe and the banana royale.

On her way back to the parking lot, strolling by the area where people sat on benches to talk and gaze at the water, she overheard a rich, masculine laugh that caught her attention. She turned to find the source of the sound and stopped when she spotted the man. He had dark-brown hair, a chiseled face, and a lean, athletic build. His profile looked vaguely familiar. Where had she seen him?

She retrieved her phone from her purse and looked up Michelle's profile on Facebook. The man's picture showed up in her featured photos section. Juliana gasped. It was Logan.

When she glanced up, the woman in his company sat next to him and acted very friendly, leaning in to speak. Logan let out another melodious laugh. She touched his arm and grasped his hands. She was a bit too friendly.

Juliana stepped closer to where Logan sat with the woman with curly, honey-blonde hair, a pale complexion, and a svelte but curvy figure that perfectly filled out her blue blazer and pencil skirt. Her slender legs were crossed and leaning toward Logan's legs. And those looked like designer pumps on her feet.

Juliana stood by a tree and pretended she was taking pictures of the water and scenery when she pointed her phone in Logan's direction. She snapped two photos of Logan and the lady before slipping her phone back into her purse. She turned and scurried in the direction of the parking lot.

Once in her car, she rested the bag of food on the passenger's seat, leaned back, and clutched the steering wheel. What was she going to tell

Michelle? She thought Logan was Michelle's boyfriend, so why was he so close and friendly with that mystery woman?

Maybe Michelle and Logan were still in the dating phase and had not defined their relationship yet? So maybe if Michelle knew that Logan might be seeing another woman, she wouldn't be hurt?

Juliana stared at the brown bag on the passenger's seat then gazed straight ahead. This was not the kind of surprise she wanted to bring. She inhaled deeply before turning on her ignition and shifting the car gear into drive. But she wouldn't be a good friend if she kept this to herself.

She had to tell Michelle.

~*~

Michelle covered her face and rubbed her temples. She raised her head and glanced around her studio. Noon, and she had just met another deadline, a difficult feat with customers coming in and out during the day. Good for business but very frustrating when she had work to do and her staff took lunch breaks.

Her stomach grumbled. She always skipped breakfast and lunch when she had a series of deadlines to meet, and today was no different. Maybe she should grab a bite? She rose from her seat and unlocked her door. When she entered the waiting area, she noticed no customers were there, so she flipped the Open sign to Closed. Whether she decided to eat or not, she needed some alone time.

"Going to lunch?" Sophia, her receptionist, jolted Michelle from her thoughts.

"I didn't know you were still here."

Sophia gave Michelle a puzzled look. "Of course I am. I'm the receptionist, and it's open business hours. You walked right by me. Are you okay?"

"Yes. Deadlines. You know."

Sophia nodded. "I see you flipped the sign. Are you having lunch now?"

"I don't know, but you're welcome to take your break."

Sophia beamed. "Okay." She grabbed her purse from behind the receptionist desk and exited the building.

Just as Michelle was about to lock the door, Juliana jogged up. What was she doing here? And with a big bag from Sofi's Crepes in her grasp. Michelle's stomach rumbled again. Did Juliana bring food? God bless the girl.

"Amiga!" Juliana gave Michelle a big hug and threw Michelle off balance.

She regained her footing and stepped back. "Good to see you, girl. What are you doing here?"

Juliana glanced around the studio. "Are we the only ones here?"

"Yes. Why?"

"Good. I need to talk to you, but first we need to eat. I bought your favorite brunch. Surprise!" Michelle reached for the bag, her mouth-watering. "We can eat in the employee break room. Follow me."

Once at the table, Michelle opened the bag and inhaled the sweet aroma of bananas, butterscotch, and crepes mixed with the savory scents of veggies and cheese. She placed the food on the table and turned to Juliana. "What's for me and what's for you?"

Juliana separated the four paper-wrapped items after reading the labels. "I bought the same order for both of us. We each have a veggie crepe and a banana royale."

Michelle bit into the veggie crepe, savoring every bite. After finishing it, she downed half of her bottle of water then turned to Juliana. "Tell me."

Juliana gave Michelle an alarmed look. "Tell you what?"

"Whatever you're not telling me. I love that you surprised me with my favorite food for brunch and that you're here, but why aren't you at work?"

"My boss gave me today off. And I know you don't eat when you're on deadline, so I thought I'd drop by and surprise you."

"But you said you had something to tell me."

Juliana cast her hazel eyes downward. "I don't know if I should tell you."

Michelle picked up her sweet crepe. "Tell me and hurry, because lunch hour will be over before we know it." She took a bite. "Mmm…delicious."

Juliana sighed. "I saw Logan…with another woman."

Michelle coughed, reached for her water, and gulped it down. "What? Where? When? How did you know it was him?"

Juliana crumpled the paper wrapper. "Today, when I was leaving Sofi's Crepes, I saw him sitting on a bench by the water with a woman. She was young, pretty, and acting very friendly, if you know what I mean."

Michelle's mind raced, but she was determined to play it cool, so she shrugged. "Probably just one of his friends or even his sister or cousin or whatever."

"You met his family?"

"Well, no. But I mean. Oh Jules, don't read too deep into whatever you saw. I'm sure it's nothing serious."

Juliana reached for her cell phone, tapped the screen a few times, then thrust it into Michelle's face. "This is what I saw."

Michelle leaned in and studied the picture. Juliana was right. The woman had clear skin, honey-blonde hair, and was petite. She also looked almost flirty as she touched Logan's arm and held his hand. She was smiling. Though Michelle hated to admit it, Juliana may be right. Maybe Logan was dating another woman.

Michelle turned her attention to her food. "Well it's not like we're an exclusive couple. We haven't defined our relationship yet. He's free to play the field." She stabbed the remainder of her crepe with a fork as her face heated and her eyes watered.

Juliana reached out and touched Michelle's hand. "I didn't want to tell you—"

"No. It's good that you told me. I needed to know, really." Michelle removed her hand from Juliana's gentle grasp. She packed up her lunch and stood. "I need to get back to work."

"But you didn't finish your sweet crepe."

Michelle's heart dropped. Why might Logan choose another woman over her? Clearly, the woman in the photo was very pretty. She looked smart and business minded, too, in her sharp, blue power suit.

Michelle's loved ones told her she was gorgeous, but there was one defining feature that the curly blonde-haired woman in the picture had that Michelle didn't—a fair skin tone.

Was her budding potential for romance over before it even started?

"I'm not hungry," she mumbled before taking the remainder of her food and throwing it in the trashcan. "You're welcome to stay here and finish eating before leaving, but I really need to return to my office."

"Michelle, it's me, your best friend. You don't have to walk away. I'm here for you. Let's talk."

Michelle steeled. "I think we've talked enough for today. Later, Jules." She rushed out of the break room, ran into her office, shut the door behind her, and collapsed on the couch.

The she buried her head in a pillow and cried.

Chapter 10

Logan dialed Michelle's number and placed the phone to his ear. It rang four times then went to voicemail. He sighed and, deciding not to leave another message, he ended the call. Two weeks had passed since he last saw or spoke to Michelle. He'd called her at least once a day for the past fourteen days, but she was not taking or returning his phone calls.

He finger-combed his hair. Why was she avoiding him? What had he said or done to upset her?

Women were a mystery.

Logan's phone rang. His heart leapt. Maybe that was Michelle. But he deflated when he saw who it was. "Hey, Sally."

"Hey, Logan. Ready for today's session?"

Normally they met an hour before lunch. "Sure. But aren't we early?"

"Yes. But I have exciting news for you, so I thought we could meet now. Can I swing by?"

"Sure. Come on over."

~*~

Michelle focused on editing pictures from her latest engagement photo shoot. She'd been throwing herself into her work and ignoring Logan's calls for the past two weeks. Seeing his picture with the pretty blonde unearthed her insecurities of not being enough, because she was a woman of color in a world where the European beauty standard was dominant. It was part of the reason why she was so passionate about featuring her clients of color on mainstream bridal magazines. The world needed to know that beauty and elegance comes in all colors.

But the cozy picture featuring Logan and the mystery woman had delivered a strong blow to her self-esteem. Maybe Marcel was right. Maybe Logan was not the type of man she should be dating. Maybe he was just using her, a fling, not a long-lasting romance. Maybe he liked white girls better. He sure did seem into that woman in the picture.

She wiped away a tear and steeled herself. She was a strong black woman who could handle heartbreak. Logan wasn't the only fish in the sea. God would send her a man who would be wonderful. *More wonderful than Logan?*

Her heart ached. Maybe she should call him. After all, he'd called her at least once a day for the past two weeks. He was probably clueless as to why she was avoiding him. But if he truly wanted her, why hadn't he stopped by her studio? He'd visited here before. It wasn't like he didn't know where to find her. She snorted as she recalled a famous adage that if a man wasn't pursuing you then it was because he was just not that into you.

But Logan had been calling every day.

Okay, God. I know I have been a bit mean by ignoring Logan's calls. But Lord, He really hurt me. You know how I don't date a lot. A guy like Logan who's interested in me seemed too good to be true. Then again, we're not official yet, so if he wants to date other women, then I shouldn't be mad. Right?

Maybe she should return his calls. But before she could dial his number, her phone rang. "Hello?"

"Hey, amiga. I know you're still mad at me, but I have good news."

"I'm not mad at you, Juliana."

"Really? Then you've not spoken to me since our lunch surprise two weeks ago because of what?"

"Jules, it's just that, well, I needed time to think."

"Mhm. Well here's food for thought. My editor-in-chief, Brenda, wants to feature your clients on the cover of *Bridal Mode Magazine*."

The phone slipped through Michelle's hand and collided with the floor. Her heartbeat accelerated. This is what she'd always wanted. She clutched her chest and breathed in deep, trying to calm down.

"Hello?" Juliana's voice sounded faint.

Michelle bent down and retrieved her phone from the floor. She put Juliana on speaker and rested the phone on her desk. "Jules, that's such great news. When did this happen? How did it happen?"

"God. He blessed you."

Michelle jumped up and down. "Yes, He did."

She forced herself to calm down and glanced at the calendar. "What issue?"

"December."

"Seven months from now? That gives me plenty of time."

"Yes, but Brenda needs your photos before the end of today because we're on a tight deadline and her original photographer could not deliver. I already shared the link to your website with her. She's interested in the photo galleries for two of your clients."

Michelle felt giddy. Her dreams were coming true.

"Which ones, Jules?"

Juliana answered.

"Great. I'll look it up now and e-mail the galleries to you."

"Gracias, amiga! Ciao!"

"Juliana, wait."

"Yes?"

"I'm really sorry that I haven't been in touch. I had a lot on my mind."

"Sure. I understand."

"We should catch up."

"Yes, we should."

"Maybe we can meet in Bowie this weekend? I can come visit you."

"Sure. We can do that."

"Okay, girl. Take care. I'm working on meeting this deadline of my dreams."

Juliana chuckled. "Later, amiga."

Michelle swiveled in her chair and pumped her fists. *Dear God, You are awesome. Thank you so much for making this dream of my heart come true.*

After spending a few moments talking to God, Michelle turned to her computer to work on this dream deadline, and for the first time in two weeks, she thought of something other than Logan.

Chapter 11

"I think you're ready."

Logan recalled Sally's words. She'd stopped by his boat last week to tell him that she thought her work with him was done and she felt confident that he was ready for his second interview with Carter Wright. He'd been excited and relieved all at once. But he hadn't called Carter immediately, because he was scared. He was close to his dream coming true, and he didn't want to mess it up. So, he did what he knew was best. He made an appointment to see his mom.

"Logan, the therapist is ready to see you."

Logan slid out of his seat in the waiting area, thanked the receptionist, and walked down the hallway to his mother's office. He opened the door and smiled at the woman behind the desk. "Hey, Mom."

Mom stood and walked over to Logan. She gave him a hug. "Hey, honey." She stepped back and gestured to the couch. "Have a seat."

Logan settled into the plush, black leather couch while his mother sat in the chair across from him.

"What's wrong?"

Logan's eyes widened. "Nothing's wrong. I just wanted to tell you this good news in person."

Mom nodded.

"Remember when I told you that I had an interview with WJLA three weeks ago?"

"Yes."

"And that I started stuttering while talking to the news director, but instead of ending the interview and dismissing me, he gave me the business card to one of his vocal coach consultants?"

"Yes."

"Well that vocal coach—her name is Sally—and I have been working together every weekday, and she told me last Friday she thinks I'm ready."

Logan watched his Mom's eyes light up with joy.

"Oh, sweetie. That's such good news. Are you going to be on air?"

Logan chuckled. "I hope so. But I've got to see if Carter Wright—he's the news director—hires me first."

"Oh, honey. I think he will." Mom paused. She frowned. "Now what's worrying your mind?"

"What do you mean?"

"I can tell that something's bothering you."

"How?"

"Mother's intuition. Is this about a girl?"

Logan sighed. "Yes."

Mom reached for a bottle of water that was resting on the end table. She twisted the cap off of the bottle and sipped before speaking. "Tell me."

"Well, Mom. I met this girl. She's amazing. We were dating for a while but never made our relationship official. Then all of a sudden, three weeks ago, she stopped talking to me. Completely. Won't take my calls. Hasn't stopped by my boat—"

"She's been on your boat?"

Logan felt his face flush. "Yes. Our first date was dinner on the boat."

Mom smiled. "Romantic."

"She seemed impressed and she... Mom she's not like any other girl I've ever dated. She's so caring and sweet, and she's compassionate about my stuttering."

"Compassionate?"

Logan nodded. "She had a cousin who stuttered. He was bullied a lot and ended up committing suicide."

Mom's eyes misted. "So sad."

"I know. But apparently, that's why Michelle is so understanding."

"She sounds like a keeper."

Logan sighed. "We haven't defined our relationship yet."

"Why not?"

"I was going to call her after my first meeting with Sally and arrange a date then ask her to be my girlfriend. But that's when she stopped taking my calls."

"Oh, honey. I'm sorry. Do you know why?"

"No. That's why I wanted to ask you. What is going on in her head?"

Mom chuckled. "How do you expect me to

know that?"

"You're a therapist. You can understand minds better than me."

Mom continued to chuckle.

"Mom, I'm serious."

Mom wiped tears that had escaped her eyes from laughing so hard.

"I wish I could help you, but I never met the girl. However, based on what you're telling me, I'd say don't give up. If she's as amazing as you say, and she truly cares about you, then I'm sure you two can work it out."

"But that's just it, Mom. I don't know what to work out, because I don't why she's mad at me."

"Ah. I see. Have you tried asking God about it?"

Logan paused. He had not prayed about this. Sure, he'd vented to God, but he hadn't asked Him for wisdom and help. Logan smiled. He got up. "Thanks, Mom. I will."

Mom glanced at her watch. "You have at least ten more minutes before my next client arrives. Are you sure you want to leave now?"

Logan kissed his mom on her right temple. "Yes, Mom. Thanks for your help."

Mom stood. "You're welcome, honey. I'm here if you ever need to talk."

"I know. You're the best."

"And when you work things out with Michelle, bring her by the house sometime. I'd love to meet her."

Logan's heart leapt. It meant a lot to him that he might have his mother's approval. He never had her approval with London. The thought of his ex-fiancée startled him. He tried not to show it. "Later, Mom."

He walked calmly out of her office and took a deep breath of the cool air when he stepped outside. *London*. The woman who broke his heart when she chose to chase her modeling dreams over creating a life with him. Marriage and family had not been a dream London wanted to pursue, apparently not even with him.

Logan looked up into the clear blue skies. *Dear God, I thought I'd never get over London. Then you sent Michelle into my life and healed my heart. Mom never liked London. But I loved her until she dumped me. I thought I was over her, but maybe I'm not? Oh, Lord. Help me work things out with Michelle and banish London from my mind. She wasn't good for me. But Michelle is someone I want to keep.*

Chapter 12

Michelle bent over and huffed. A few yards ahead, Juliana turned around and jogged in place. She rallied Michelle in a military-boot-camp-leader voice. "Let's go, amiga! No breaks."

Michelle raised her head just high enough to glare at Juliana. "You said we were going for a walk in the park, not a run."

Juliana gave a rich peal of laughter in response. She jogged back to Michelle's side and slapped her on her upper back. "You need to look fit for this shoot in Italy. You never know when you're going to meet a cute guy. Maybe your second shooter for the wedding will turn out to be Mr. Right."

Michelle winced, partly because Juliana's hand slap hurt and partly because the comment got her thinking of Logan, who she hadn't spoken to now in many months.

As if reading her mind, Juliana frowned. Her voice softened. "I'm sorry. I didn't mean to make you think of Lo—"

Michelle raised her hand and stood up straight. "It's okay. I'm over him. And you're right. I could meet Mr. Right in Italy. So, let's get this run done." She willed her conflicted emotions away. *Dear God, please don't let Juliana bring his name up again. I've tried so hard to get over Logan, but sometimes the sound of his name still makes my heart hurt. I miss him so much. But this is my fault. I stopped taking his calls, and now it looks like he's given up.*

Juliana jogged alongside Michelle. For a few moments, she remained silent, and all Michelle could hear was the pounding of their feet on the pavement.

Juliana puffed. "I'm happy for you, amiga. Look at you getting all geared up to photograph your first international wedding. Can you believe how fast this is happening?"

"Yes. It feels like I just received the phone call yesterday." A lot had happened in the past two months. After having her clients on the cover of *Bridal Mode Magazine*, Michelle's phone had been ringing off the hook with requests from magazine editors across the U.S. and then most recently, in Paris and Milan.

That feature led to the opportunity of a lifetime. Maria Ricci, the editor of *Bella Bride Magazine* in Italy, had reached out to Michelle a few weeks ago. She had gushed about Michelle's photography and shared the photos with her daughter who told her that she wanted Michelle to be her wedding photographer.

Juliana's voice bubbled. "I think it's awesome

how you're saving the day, their wedding day."

Michelle huffed as she tried to maintain Juliana's pace. The girl had legs of steel. "It's not about me. God worked behind the scenes."

Normally wedding photographers booked their clients months in advance, but Maria said that her daughter's original wedding photographer had a last-minute scheduling conflict, and since she admired Michelle's work so much, it only made sense to hire her.

"I cannot believe you're going to stay in a real villa on the Amalfi Coast."

Michelle paused to stretch and catch her breath. "Maria's the best. She's covering everything."

Juliana jogged circles around Michelle who was still stretching. "You're going to have the time of your life." Juliana pulled on Michelle's arm. "Let's keep going. We're almost there." She pointed to the end of the trail that circled back to the beginning.

"Good. I'm thirsty. And hungry."

"Me too. Good thing the town center is only a mile away."

"We've got another mile to go?"

"Yep. We're going to be so fit we're going to be asked to be magazine cover models like your clients."

Michelle hugged Juliana.

"What was that for?"

"A thank you for allowing God to use you to help my career dreams come true."

"You're welcome, but I only played a small role. Everything after your cover on *Bridal Mode Magazine* was thanks to God and God alone."

"You're right, and I'm so grateful to Him."

"Race you to lunch at Marie's Mocha?"

"You're on."

Juliana took off toward the café, and Michelle followed at a slower pace. Twenty-four hours until her flight left. After lunch, she had to pack. Her stomach danced around. What if something went wrong? What if she lost her luggage or if she dropped her camera? What if the pictures didn't turn out how she wanted them to look?

This could be wonderful.

It could be a disaster.

~*~

London Lane paused on the cobblestone Parisian street. A stunning couple on an American bridal magazine cover at the newsstand commanded her attention.

The bride glowed with an olive complexion and dark brown tresses that cascaded down her shoulders, and the groom had skin the color of mocha and the body build of an athlete. He cradled her waist and kissed her forehead. Her eyes were closed, and a soft smile graced her face. The photo was captivating. The couple was gorgeous and complemented each other perfectly.

She'd hire this photographer for her wedding.

London purchased the magazine, meandered a few steps to the patio of a cozy little café, and sat at a table for two. She flipped through the magazine to find out the name of the wedding photographer for future reference. After a few minutes, she hit pay dirt. Michelle Hadley.

Since she hadn't heard of her before, she

searched for that name. What a surprise. Michelle was a young, black wedding photographer based in Annapolis, Maryland.

She must be pretty good to have photos of her clients on a mainstream magazine in France. She needed to book this girl for her wedding.

London rubbed the diamond on her ring finger and gazed at it. She never should have broken up with Logan two years ago. He'd been so hurt, but he wouldn't let her give back the ring.

If she had stayed with Logan, she would just have been London Lane, the pretty wife of Logan Emerson. But because of her decision to follow her dreams, she was a model who graced the covers of local and international fashion magazines. She'd made enough money to last her a lifetime. But something, or rather someone, was missing from her life. And she was determined to get him back.

London picked up her phone and dialed her manager.

"Charlie, I need two weeks of me time."

"Why, darling?"

"I have unfinished business in the United States."

"You can have the two weeks if you promise to do some photo shoots for magazines while there. I can arrange that for you."

"Deal."

"Let me work on your schedule. When do you want to leave?"

"Tomorrow."

"I'll get the private jet ready."

"Thanks, Charlie."

"Anything for you, my dear."

London ended the call and smiled. She kissed her ring.

Logan, here I come.

Chapter 13

Logan read the teleprompter. His words were well enunciated, his tone was professional, and for several months, his stuttering hadn't shown up and ruined the show. Maybe God had cured him or at least answered his prayers to keep his stuttering inactive while he was on-air.

Jimmy Moreno, the floor manager inside WJLA's studio, gave Logan the sign to let him know that they were off-air for the commercial break. "Great job."

He grinned at the floor manager who had rooted for him since day one on the job. "Thank you."

Jimmy nodded. "You're back on in two minutes."

Logan reached beneath his desk for his water bottle. Staying hydrated helped keep his vocal chords functioning properly. He took a sip and gazed around the studio. Carter had hired Logan immediately after his voice lessons ended. He gave Logan an anchor job, because he felt he was ready for the challenge.

Logan prayed every day to make a good impression on his boss and the viewers, and so far, God had been answering his prayer. The viewers loved Logan—especially female viewers. Since joining WJLA, Logan's professional Twitter account gained over ten thousand followers. He had hit his career stride and could only go up from here.

"You're on in five…four…"

At the sound of Jimmy's prompting, Logan finished his last sip of water and returned the bottle to its position on the floor below his anchor desk. He cleared his throat and stared straight into his teleprompter.

Jimmy gave the sign that Logan was on air, and the words started scrolling. Logan spoke clearly and confidently about the new community center when something and someone caught his eye.

A woman.

A diamond.

Logan blinked. What was London doing here?

She smiled and waved.

Logan stumbled over his words.

Oh God, not now. Please.

As if time was in his favor, the teleprompter instructed Logan to go to commercial break. He tried his best to regain his composure, but it was too late. He tried not to show his distress on his face as he read the words.

"W-w-we w-will b-b-be right b-b-back."

Jimmy gave the sign that they were off-air. He studied Logan and shook his head. "You all right, man?"

Logan nodded. He pulled at his tie. Why did it feel hot?

He gulped his water and gazed at the spot where London stood. He was not imagining her. He adjusted his collar and tried not to stare, but she was even more gorgeous than when she broke his heart and left him for her modeling career in Europe.

And that ring. The bling was blinding. Was it the same one he'd given her and refused to take back when she broke up with him? Or was she engaged to someone else? But why would she show up now, and how did she get access to the studio?

"Logan, you're on in five."

He averted his eyes to the ceiling, nodded, and prayed for composure. *Dear God, please help me to get it together.*

Jimmy gave the sign that Logan was on-air. He regained his composure, smiled at the cameras, and to his mortification, continued to stumble over his words as he read the teleprompter. He prayed that this wouldn't cost him his job. He would talk to London as soon as this broadcast ended and get to the bottom of why she was here. Why now?

~*~

"I missed you, Logan."

Logan set his jaw. He was trying not to show his anger, but London made him stutter on air after five weeks of incident-free newscasts. He could lose his job. After the show, Logan had walked over to London. She gave him a warm hug and kissed his left cheek, acting like they never broke up. He took her by her elbow and guided her to the exit. He told the receptionist that he and his guest were going on a lunch break. Fifteen minutes later, they sat at a table for two in the restaurant that was in the same building as WJLA's studio.

"Why are you here? Why now? How did you even get into the studio?"

London reached across the table and closed her hands over his. "Because I missed you, love. And I got in because I know people."

Logan withdrew his hands. He gave a slow, disbelieving shake of his head. "I don't understand. You wanted the freedom to chase your career dreams. You broke up with me."

London toyed with the diamond on her ring finger. "Yes, I did. But I needed to make my career dreams come true, and they did. But lately, I've been thinking. We were good together, Logan. I would like to recapture what we had."

He said nothing but focused on the ring. He recognized it as the one that he had customized for her. "Why are you still wearing that?"

She smiled coyly. "Because I'm hoping we can keep our engagement?"

He shook his head and finger-combed his hair then slapped his hands on the table. "You left me for your career. Didn't talk to me for two years, and now you want me to take you back? Resume our engagement and get married?"

"It's worth a try, right?"

For a moment, he stared at her. Two years ago, this would be the situation he'd hoped for but now... Now he had met Michelle. They hadn't spoken in months, but she had made a lasting impression on his heart. She was so much kinder and more caring than London. She was brilliant, beautiful, and a good businesswoman. Most of all, she didn't get turned off by his stuttering. His speech impediment used to annoy London.

"You surprised me today," Logan said. "I hadn't stuttered in weeks."

London nodded. She reached for his hand. "I know. I'm sorry, sweetie."

Logan raised his eyebrow. She wasn't fazed by his stuttering? This was new. Maybe she had changed. But was it worth giving her another chance? And what about Michelle? They hadn't spoken in months.

London's hazel eyes shone bright with hope. Her sleek, honey-blonde hair flowed from her crown to her shoulders. Her light tan made her glow. Her skin was flawless, and her red lips were pursed in a perfect pout. She reached into her purse and pulled out a business card.

"Here's my new number. Think about it and call me with your decision. I'm in town on business for two weeks."

Logan glanced at the business card and then at London. "I can't promise I'll call you."

London smiled. "I know, love. But I hope you will." She picked up her purse, stood, and kissed Logan's right cheek. Without speaking a word, she left.

Logan grabbed a napkin and wiped both of his cheeks. He didn't want any contact with her. He picked up the business card, and for a moment, he was tempted to tear it in two. But then his heart softened. At one time in his life, he was ready to marry her. Now she was back and hinting that she'd changed. Maybe he should give her a second chance.

Chapter 14

Michelle paused at the airport entrance. She held her luggage tighter and surveyed the scene in front of her. People busied about, luggage in tow. Some rushed past her into the airport, about to board their flight out of Italy. Others strolled past her outdoors, on their cell phones or simply looking like they were basking in the sunshine while waiting for their ride.

As Michelle stood still, she tried to gather her emotions. *Wow. I'm actually in Italy. I cannot believe it. I am going to photograph my clients in one of the most romantic destinations on earth.*

Despite the sixteen-hour flight, Michelle was ultra-awake and ready to seize the day. Her attention turned to the cars pulling to the curb. Maria said she was sending her nephew Nico to pick Michelle up at the airport and drive her to their villa.

She inhaled deeply, prayed to God to calm her nerves, and moved forward. The automatic doors slid open, and the cool breeze whipped through her hair while the sun kissed her skin. She restrained herself from dancing for joy.

Watching the sunrise over the ocean through the window from inside her seat in first class was the first romantic experience for Michelle during this trip. Since she was in the most romantic country, she expected more beautiful experiences. Maybe Juliana was right. She just might get an Italian boyfriend. Whatever she and Logan had was gone, and it was time to move on. However, she did recall her conversation with Juliana at the café after their jog in the park. Juliana quietly mentioned that when it came to Logan, Michelle still got that faraway look in her eyes.

Michelle shook her head. That was then, this was now. Her mama taught her the importance of living each day in the present and not dwelling on the past. She was going to enjoy every moment of this new adventure. She reached into her purse and retrieved her English to Italian language translation book. The glossy pages flipped easily as she looked up a greeting and smiled. She shut the book, held her arms open wide and greeted the people in the language of the land. *"Ciao, bella Italia!"*

Several people stopped and waved at her, returning her greeting with a friendly smile and *"ciao"*. Michelle's heart warmed. She almost felt at home.

The wind whipped through her hair as she walked to the pick-up lane and waited patiently in line with other travelers who were hailing taxis. A man who looked like a dark-haired, olive-skinned,

Italian version of the famous American actor Matthew McConaughey stepped out of his fire-red Lamborghini and stood out above the crowd. He made eye contact with Michelle and flashed a bright smile that revealed book-perfect teeth and waved.

"Buongiorno, signorina!"

Michelle smiled, waved, then continued waiting. *People sure are friendly here. I love it. But I don't think that I know that man.* Seconds later, the man stood by her side. She jumped and turned to face him. "Yes?"

He chuckled and extended his right hand.

"I'm Nico Ricci. Maria's nephew. I am your second shooter for the wedding. You are Michelle Hadley, no?"

Michelle shook his hand. "Yes, I am. How did you know my name?"

"Facebook and my Aunt Maria's bridal magazines."

Michelle narrowed her eyes as she recognized the man. Her cheeks warmed. How could she not notice him before? This was Maria's nephew. She saw his photo on his photography business website. He was much more dashing in person, a rarity. She extended her right hand. "I'm sorry, Nico. I didn't recognize you at first. It's a pleasure to meet you."

Nico accepted her hand but instead of shaking it, he raised it to his lips and kissed it. He then smiled at her. "Always a pleasure to meet another wedding photographer as *bella*—that means beautiful—as you."

Suddenly, she felt very shy. "Thanks," she murmured. She withdrew her hand from his firm yet gentle grasp and reached for her luggage.

He maneuvered around her and within seconds had all her luggage in his grasp except for her purse and camera bag. He smiled, revealing his perfectly aligned, pearly-white teeth. Michelle's heart fluttered. He had a great smile, and he was very good looking, but she was determined not to make their time together anything but professional. If God wanted to send her an Italian boyfriend, it would have to happen after the wedding.

Nico spoke, interrupting her private thoughts. He tilted his head toward where his car was parked. "Shall we?"

Michelle nodded and followed his lead. "We shall."

~*~

"Here we are. Wake up, *bella* Michelle."

Michelle's eyes slowly fluttered open. She yawned and stretched. She hadn't meant to fall asleep in the passenger's seat of Nico's unbelievably hot ride, but jet lag had gotten the best of her. So, after a ten-minute conversation with Nico, she'd fallen asleep. She glanced at her watch. It was an hour later, and they'd just arrived at the most beautiful villa Michelle had seen.

Nico parked his car on the street next to the pathway that led to the front door of the villa. He turned to Michelle and smiled. "Welcome to my home."

She took in the glorious scenery before her eyes. The villa was elegant, three stories tall, and set on the waterfront. She could almost feel the beach that looked like it was only a few hundred feet away.

The fresh air and saltwater scent of the sea wafted to her nose. She inhaled deeply as she tilted her head upward. Her gaze fixed on the balcony with rose-colored rails that wrapped around the second and third stories of the villa painted in a deep shade of cream. There were four arched windows with sea blue shutters on each story of the villa.

She turned to Nico. "You live here?"

He chuckled. "Yes. I live with my Aunt Maria and her husband Giovanni. Nice, huh?"

"Breathtaking."

Nico unlocked the doors. He got out of the car and popped the trunk. As he retrieved Michelle's luggage, she forced herself to stop staring and exit the car. She slipped her purse over one shoulder and her favorite Ona camera bag over the other then placed her feet that were comfortably clad in memory-foam ballet flats on the smooth blue pavement.

Nico had already started toward the front door. She picked up her pace and followed him. A moment later, the door flew open, and there was a petite but curvy woman with silky black hair that perfectly framed her face in loose curls. The woman had a radiant smile, beige skin, and blue eyes that sparkled like the sea. Michelle identified the woman, Maria Ricci, from their Skype conversations about the wedding plans.

Maria kissed Nico on his right and left cheeks then did the same to Michelle.

"*Ciao*, my loves!"

Michelle drew back. She wasn't used to such enthusiasm and affectionate greetings, but the woman's gusto reminded her of Juliana's way of interacting with people. She made a mental note to call Juliana after she got settled in. Her stomach grumbled, and the woman laughed. "We're going to eat lunch soon."

Michelle blushed and averted her eyes to the larger-than-life pink roses that lined the walkway.

The woman extended her hand to Michelle. "It's so wonderful to meet you in person."

She shook Maria's hand. "You too. Thanks for opening your home to me. It is, how do you say *en Italiano? Molto bella.*"

Maria's eyed danced, and she clapped with joy. "It is so delightful to hear you speak our language." She looped her left arm through Michelle's right and ushered her into the home. Nico followed. "I'll show you to your room. Nico will leave your bags there, and you can freshen up before lunch."

As they climbed the stairs, Michelle noted how every decorative detail of the house said Mediterranean. The deep blue carpet, white walls, and glossy white marble floors. Even the tan leather couches, country-style tables, and plush rose-pink chairs looked warm and inviting.

Maria opened the door and let go of Michelle's arm. "This is our guest suite. Fresh sheets are on the bed. Make yourself at home. Lunch will be served outdoors on our patio overlooking the coast. It's downstairs in the back. If you need help finding it, just call out to me. I have very good hearing."

Michelle smiled. "Thanks, Maria. I appreciate your hospitality."

"It is my pleasure."

Nico walked into the room and placed Michelle's luggage on the floor next to the queen-sized bed. He smiled at Michelle. "If you need me, just call my name. I have good hearing too."

Nico and Maria laughed in unison. Michelle smiled. She liked the warmth of this family. They put her at ease. But she still needed time with Nico to establish a rapport before they worked together at the wedding. She turned to him as he exited her room. "Nico?"

He stopped. "Yes?"

"Can we talk about the wedding? I know we have all day tomorrow to scout the area, but I really need to get a feel for how we're going to work together."

Nico reached out and rested his right hand on her right arm. He gave it a reassuring squeeze. "Don't worry, princess. This is not my first, how do you Americans say, rodeo?"

Michelle sighed. "I know. I've seen your photography website. It's very impressive, but we still need to time to talk and scout the area."

"My lady, we will do all of that tomorrow. Today we eat and enjoy life. Tomorrow we can work out the details. Deal?"

Michelle bit her lip. It was no point starting an argument over this, so she acquiesced. After all, they did have all day tomorrow to interact and travel up and down the Amalfi Coast as they prepared for their clients' wedding. She looked Nico squarely in his eyes, hoping that her standing in a strong, power stance with folded arms conveyed that she meant business. She made sure that the tone of her voice was even before speaking. "Deal."

Nico chuckled. "See you outside for lunch soon." With that, he disappeared down the long hallway. Michelle listened to his footfalls descend the stairs before returning to her room. She shut the door behind her and threw herself on the bed. Jet lag was no joke. She was sure that Maria wouldn't mind if she rested before eating. Michelle snuggled with the purple, lavender-scented pillows and closed her eyes. She inhaled deeply. The scent was so relaxing. She could get used to this. As she drifted off, she thought how lovely it would be if Logan were here to share this experience. Italy was so beautiful. He'd love it here. She'd love it if he were here. If only they were still talking to each other. He was slowly but surely becoming the one man she could not forget.

Chapter 15

A knock at the door woke Michelle from her slumber. She opened her eyes and squinted at the glare of the bright yet beautiful sunlight that flooded her room. The refreshing scent of ocean air and cool breeze filled the room. She sat up straight. "Yes?"

The door opened by a few inches, and Nico peeked in. "May I come in?"

She smoothed her hair and adjusted her shirt. She'd slept on top of her bed in her clothes from yesterday. She yawned. Hopefully that was the last of the jet lag. "Yes. Come in."

Nico opened the door wide and entered. He was holding a breakfast tray. Her stomach rumbled at the sight of food. Nico chucked. "Since you slept through lunch and dinner last night, I brought you, how do you Americans say? Breakfast in bed."

Michelle chuckled. She accepted the tray that Nico placed on her lap. "Thanks." She studied the food then sampled a slice of the fresh oranges and enjoyed the tangy, citrus taste. She inhaled the roasted coffee beans and poured cream into the cup of coffee before taking a sip and diving into the ciabatta. She paused between bites to speak. "The food tastes delicious. Did you make it?"

Nico sat down in the chair by the desk across from the bed. "No. We have a chef. Her name is Carissa. She's good, no?"

Michelle's mouth was full, so she nodded and gave Nico a thumbs-up.

He chuckled. "I'll let you enjoy your food. We leave in twenty minutes." He stood and walked toward the door.

She swallowed and sipped some coffee before talking. "Twenty minutes? Where are we going?"

"You wanted to scout locations for the wedding tomorrow, no?"

"Yes. I did. Still do."

"Good. I'm ready when you are."

She gave him another thumbs up, and he left. She picked up her pace in finishing her breakfast. Five minutes later, she was finished, and in another ten, she was ready to go.

Now fully dressed, she picked up her camera, stepped onto the balcony and gazed at the panoramic waterfront view. She took pictures of everything. The ocean waves rose to the shore then receded back into their depths. People relaxed along the beach. Couples strolled hand in hand. Children chased seagulls and built sandcastles.

Maybe it was because of her West Indian heritage from her dad, but there was nothing like being under water. It rejuvenated her spirit and soothed her soul. She made a mental note to visit her extended family in Barbados soon. Now that she was in Italy and near their gorgeous beaches, maybe she'd satisfy her craving after the wedding by spending time on the beach and in the ocean off the Amalfi Coast. She lived and worked not far from the Chesapeake Bay in Annapolis, but the water there was not as clear as the water here or on her dad's island home. She looked forward to discovering Italy.

~*~

Michelle held tight to Nico's waist as they drove his Vespa into Ravello from the city of Amalfi. The small scooter made her nervous. Thankfully, Nico was not speeding, but still, she'd be relieved when they stopped. As if reading her thoughts, Nico pulled to the side of the road where a few other Vespas were parked.

Michelle removed her helmet and got off. She ran a hand through her tresses to avoid helmet hair. Today, she'd left her purse at home and only slipped her wallet and cell phone into a side compartment of her classy camera bag. She didn't want to be weighed down while traveling through town.

Nico pocketed his keys, adjusted his camera bag, then turned to Michelle. "Ready for a hike?"

Michelle glanced at her soft-pink ballerina flats. They were comfortable but nowhere near durable for a hike. "What do you mean?"

"I thought we could park here then walk up the hill to the church where we're shooting the wedding. Then we can walk into town. It will only take about fifteen minutes. After sightseeing and grabbing an early dinner, we can drive to see more of the coast."

"Okay."

Nico stretched out his arms as if embracing the atmosphere. "Welcome to Ravello."

She marveled at the scenery of this coastal town. The deep, pure blue of the water only rivaled the clear blue sky. The pink, purple, red, and orange flowers gave a feminine touch to this work of everyday art. The greenery was abundant, covering the hills and enhancing the sides of the buildings on the land. The pavement was smooth and only rugged around the edges.

Nico started toward the church on the hill, and she followed. Nico glanced over his shoulder. "The church doors should be open. I know the priest. He's always here."

Michelle picked up her pace. "Great."

Moments later, they stood in front of big sea-blue door. Nico pushed the door open, and they stepped inside the church and paused in awe. The walls were painted in a smooth, cream color with a hue of orange mixed with a soft yellow glow. The carpet was a rich shade of deep blue. The pews were perfectly crafted with glossy wood and ample, plush, golden cushions. As she peered heavenward, she caught sight of the beautiful stained-glass window that featured angels in red, blue, and yellow glass.

"Welcome to San Francesco Church. It was built by Saint Francis of Assisi in the thirteenth century and rebuilt in the eighteenth century. It can hold up to one hundred wedding guests. Isn't it exquisite?"

"Molta bella."

Nico chuckled. "Is that the only Italian phrase you studied?"

"Maybe."

"Don't worry, I'll help you expand your vocabulary."

They wandered around inside the large and majestic foyer. Nico pointed. "So, there will be a short podium here holding a book for the guests to sign when they arrive. The bridal party will line up here, and this is where the bride will enter and walk down the aisle." Nico swung open the double doors, revealing the sanctuary.

Michelle gasped. It was gorgeous. She entered, took out her camera, and snapped a few pictures.

She pointed her lens to the cathedral's arched ceiling. After taking pictures for five minutes, she slid into a seat in the front row pew and sat still to absorb every moment of this experience.

Nico slid into the pew next to her. "I'll cover the groom's side of the church, and you cover the bride's. I'll capture the look on the groom's face when his bride enters this sanctuary, while you capture the look on her face as they see each other. Does the bride want to do a first look before the ceremony?"

"I'm used to giving the orders to my second shooter, but everything you said makes perfect sense. It's like we're on the same page. I'm looking forward to working with you."

"Me too. It's an honor to work with you. I've studied your photography online and in the magazines. You're going to be famous. I'd give it a year for it to happen. And I can humbly say that I was your second shooter for your first international wedding."

Nico's kind words warmed Michelle's heart.

He reached out and gave Michelle's left arm a reassuring squeeze. "You'll do great, *bella* Michelle."

"Thanks."

"Ready for that hike into town? Lots of sights to see and good food to eat."

"Yes. Let's go."

She followed him out of the church, and they began their short hike into the town of Ravello. Cascading cliffs with lush greenery bordered the background. Michelle took photos of every detail that inspired her—the deep pastel colors that Mediterranean architecture was known for, sleek luxury yachts and boats that were docked on the clear blue waters. She photographed window displays in the fancy boutiques that lined the narrow streets as she inhaled the sea salt scent of the air. She could live here.

Her stomach grumbled. Nico turned to her. "I always know when you need to eat. There's a nice restaurant around the corner. Let's go there." He took her by the hand and led the way.

Nico was more expressive than any male colleague that she'd worked with before. He was still the perfect gentleman, so she wasn't worried.

Moments later, they were seated at a table for two inside a quaint but cozy little restaurant that Michelle would have walked by if Nico hadn't noticed it at first. He picked up the menu. "What would you like? I can translate the menu for you."

"That won't be necessary." She opened her menu. Despite the English to Italian language guidebook, she was at a loss for words.

"Do you eat meat?"

She'd allow him to order for her. "Yes. I'd like a chicken entrée and a side of salad. Bread would be nice too."

"*Bella* Michelle, we are in Italy. Bread with dipping olive oil is always a given."

Moments later, their waiter arrived. Nico and the waiter exchanged words in Italian. After the waiter left, Nico switched back to speaking in English. "So, tell me about yourself."

"What do you want to know?"

"What made you fall in love with wedding photography? When did you know you wanted to be a wedding photographer? You have a studio back home in the States, right?"

"Yes. I have a studio in Annapolis, Maryland. It's called Love in Pictures."

The waiter returned with two tall glasses of ice water.

"I fell in love with photography at an early age. My dad bought a camera for me when I was ten. I knew then I wanted to take pictures for a living, and I've always loved weddings. So, it made sense to become a wedding photographer."

"And now you've got your first international wedding assignment *en Italia*. Exciting, isn't it?"

"Very."

They spent more time in conversation until the

food arrived. Michelle bowed her head and said a silent prayer. When she looked up, Nico was in the prayer position too. Once he opened his eyes, she cut into the lean chicken breast and savored it. Nico stabbed his steak with his fork and raised the food to his mouth. Neither spoke until they were ready to order dessert. Nico broke the silence. "When the food is good, no one wants to talk."

"So true."

"Would you like dessert?"

Michelle glanced at her watch. "Not sure. It's only 6 o'clock. Are we doing more sightseeing before we hike back to your Vespa?"

"We could, but if you want dessert, you'd better order it before we leave, because here in Italy, we close our restaurants at 7:00 p.m."

Michelle eyes widened. "Really? Why?"

"We want to spend time with our loved ones and enjoy life."

"Oh. That's nice."

"I know." He picked up the menu and flipped to the dessert section. "I'm getting the tiramisu. What would you like?"

"What you ordered sounds good."

"You've never had it?"

Michelle shook her head. Nico signaled the waiter. This time he spoke in English. "We'll have two tiramisus."

The waiter nodded and left.

Michelle felt confused. "I thought he only spoke Italian."

"Tiramisu is an Italian word."

They spent another hour at the restaurant,

enjoying their dessert and talking like old friends. On their walk back to the church, they watched the picturesque sunset. Hopefully, the wedding tomorrow would be as flawless as today with Nico. How perfect her day would have been if Logan had been here too.

Chapter 16

Logan sank back into the pillow-filled, plush blue couch inside the living area of his yacht. The sparkling water in his champagne flute swooshed ever so slightly as the water lapped against his boat. The sea breeze flowed through the windows, a welcome relief against his warm skin. He inhaled the scent of salt water. There was nothing like living on a boat in Annapolis.

He turned his attention from looking out the window to his computer and paused over his Facebook friend request notifications. London. Should he or shouldn't he add her as a friend? He hovered his mouse over her request. For a week, he'd been avoiding calling her back, and he still wasn't ready.

He'd imagined himself marrying London and starting a family with her, but that was before she broke his heart. Now when he thought about her, he didn't feel that overwhelming sense of love and desire to be there for her. But he did know the one woman who made him believe in love again, and she hadn't spoken to him in ten weeks. Not that he was counting. He went to check her page and raised his eyebrows. His body tensed.

Michelle had an entire album dedicated to her travels in Italy. It looked like she was there to photograph a wedding. He browsed through the pictures and froze when he saw a selfie of Michelle and a man. He was holding a camera too. They had matching smiles and were glowing. The caption read, "We're having so much fun! #secondshooter #firstinternationalwedding #reception #AmalfiCoast #Italy."

Logan ran his hands through his hair. Who was this guy? Michelle's colleague, given the caption. But they looked a little too friendly and happy to be strictly about business. Is this why he hadn't heard from her in ten weeks? She moved on? Logan clenched his jaw. Well, if Michelle moved on, so could he.

He confirmed London's request to be Facebook friends. He then picked up his phone and dialed her number. His hands shook out of anger. He wasn't sure that he wanted to rekindle his romance with London, but he could at least give her a chance and see if it was worth it. Logan pressed his phone to his ear. It rang three times. London picked it up on the fourth ring.

"Hello?"

"H-h-hey L-l-london. It's m-m-me." Logan clenched his free fist. He wished that being upset wasn't a trigger for his stuttering, but it happened every time.

"Oh hey, Logan! How are you?"

"G-g-great. Want to meet me for dinner?"

"I'd love to."

~*~

"So, what made you change your mind?"

Logan gazed at London across their table for two inside the airy, upscale French restaurant with a name that he could not pronounce. The interior design of the place was very country with farmhouse décor, warm colors, and wide, open spaces divided by etched glass. He weighed his words before speaking.

"We had something good. Real good."

London nodded and leaned forward. Her hazel eyes danced. "And?"

"And I'd like to see if we can get it back."

London reached across the table and grasped Logan by his hands. Her touch was gentle and firm at the same time, her slender hands like silk. "I'd like to give us another try too."

A smile tugged at the corner of his lips. "Okay."

London smiled and released her grip. "I'm flying out to Paris next week. Let's make the most of my time here."

"Agreed. You've lived there for a while now, right?"

London nodded. "Two years. I love it. You should visit me there for Christmas. Paris is so beautiful in December, especially at night. The city lights are gorgeous."

London rushed on. "You know, you don't have to if you already have plans. But I'd love for you to see the City of Love. Paris isn't beautiful by itself."

Their waitress approached the table and placed two hot plates of food on the table. *"Bon appétit!"*

Logan dipped his spoon into his French onion soup. He savored the smooth texture and rich taste. He didn't look up until he was halfway done. London stared at him. "What?"

"Nothing."

He reached for a napkin and wiped the corners of his mouth. "No. Tell me. If we want to give this another go, then we need to be open and honest with each other."

London bit her bottom lip. She averted her eyes and played with the corner of her napkin. Logan stifled a laugh. Some things never changed. This is exactly what she did when she was nervous about what she wanted to say. "It's okay. You can talk to me."

She glanced up and gave a timid smile. It was the same smile that made him fall in love with her when they first started dating. "Do you still love me?"

He cast his eyes down for a moment. "It's going to take time to rebuild what we had."

Her shoulders drooped, ruining her perfect posture, and for a moment, Logan's heart went out to her. Was it possible their breakup hurt her as much as it had hurt him?

She sat tall again and flashed a confident smile. "I'm willing to fight for us, babe."

Was he willing to fight for her? What would happen if London and Michelle were ever in the same room together with him? How would he react? Better yet, if he had the choice, which woman would he choose?

His heart knew the answer to that question.

Chapter 17

Logan and London walked hand-in-hand toward Marie's Mocha Café. She was officially restored to girlfriend status—his girlfriend—and he did not want to revisit his feelings for Michelle. They were too powerful.

He held the door open for her, and she kissed him on his lips before walking in. "Thanks, babe."

Logan sighed. He didn't have the heart to tell London that they didn't have the same spark. Whatever made him fall in love with her when they first started dating years ago had disappeared. He truly was trying to rebuild their relationship from the ground up. But was it worth it? "You're welcome, babe."

They stepped into the café and claimed their spot in line, still holding hands. Out of habit, he glanced to the left. He couldn't help it. He always looked at the corner half booth not far from the smoothie machine, because that was Michelle's spot. He looked forward to seeing her even though he shouldn't because he was with London. But he couldn't help but look.

True to habit, Michelle sat there. Logan's heart leapt then sank to his stomach, which twisted. Michelle was here, sitting in her usual place, sipping her drink while staring at her computer screen. Why wasn't she with that photographer guy in Italy? He thought she was going to stay there for a long while. Maybe he had misunderstood her status update on Facebook?

He forced himself to stop staring and move into a plan of action. He turned to London and embraced her. He whispered in her ear. "Let's go, babe. I have some place better in mind."

Then he maneuvered her out of line and out of the café. He prayed Michelle hadn't spied him.

~*~

Logan tossed the basketball to Cameron. The ball swooshed into the hoop. What Logan really needed was to talk, and Cameron was the best man to talk to about what was on his heart.

Cameron bounced the ball and traveled toward Logan. But instead of passing, he picked the ball up and held it under his arm. "What's going on, man?"

"I need to talk."

"Yeah. I figured that out five minutes ago when you missed a perfect shot. You never miss. What's going on?"

Logan walked toward the nearby bench, and Cameron followed. They sat on opposite ends and turned to talk. "London's back."

Cameron's eyes grew wide. "Your London? The girl who broke your heart?"

Logan nodded.

"Wasn't she in Europe or someplace far away?"

Another nod.

"Why is she here?"

"She wants to give us another chance."

"Us? As in you and her?" Cameron leaned forward. He spoke in a lower tone. "You're not seriously considering taking her back, are you?"

"We are back together. I'm trying to give it another go and see where it leads."

Cameron snorted. "I'll tell you where it leads. No place good. That woman is trouble."

Logan clenched his jaw. "You don't even know her."

Cameron chortled. "I know enough about her to know she's not for you. I was there when you two were dating and engaged, remember? You called me when she broke your engagement and your heart. How quickly you forget what she put you through. And you want to set yourself up for that kind of pain again? And what about Michelle? I've never seen you happier. What happened to her?"

Logan tried to calm down his accelerated heartbeat. "We're not talking."

"Why not?"

Logan explained what happened many months ago. He left out the part about seeing Michelle at the café earlier that morning. By the time Logan finished, Cameron was shaking his head. "No. It's wrong. All wrong." He held out his hand. "Let me see your phone."

Logan froze. "Why?"

"Log into Facebook and let me see that status

update from Michelle."

Logan followed orders.

Cameron laughed.

Logan frowned. "What's so funny?"

"Dude. It says here that this Italian man is her second shooter at the wedding. Do you know what that means?"

Logan shook his head. Cameron slapped him on his shoulder before speaking. "It means that he's her colleague, not her boyfriend. Man, you just let a good girl go over a stupid misunderstanding."

Logan rubbed his shoulder, which still stung from Cameron's slap. But it didn't hurt as much as his heart. Could he be wrong about Michelle? He felt sick to his stomach. Maybe he overreacted. This was not good. He had to fix this. Now. Logan stood.

Cameron looked up. "Going somewhere?"

"Yeah, man. Going to make things right with Michelle."

Cameron clapped. "That's my boy. Go get your girl."

Logan jogged to his car. Michelle sometimes worked late at her studio. Hopefully, she was still there. They needed to talk.

Chapter 18

Michelle glanced at the time on her computer screen. Eight o'clock, but she was still at work, editing the photos from the Italian wedding. What a beautiful experience filled with memorable moments and fun times sightseeing southern Italy with Nico.

By the time she was on the airplane flying home, she had made a lifetime friend in him. He understood her in ways most men did not. He truly was one-of-a-kind. He had a passionate personality and made her laugh. But as wonderful as he was, they were better off as friends. What was he up to?

Michelle hummed her favorite song from the wedding as she logged into Facebook. But the joyful tune died on her lips as she stared at a picture in her newsfeed from Logan's page. Her heart stopped, freezing her in time.

Logan was kissing a blonde woman with a sun-kissed tan, honey-blonde hair that cascaded down her shoulders to her waist, and a slender body clothed in what looked like designer apparel. But the double dagger to Michelle's heart was that the picture showed the woman's ring finger as she held his face. She stopped breathing when she saw the caption. All in caps, it read, "We're getting married!"

Michelle felt sick to her stomach. She stood and rushed to the bathroom. After throwing up for what felt like an eternity, the doorbell to her studio rang. She flushed the toilet and rose from her seat on the bathroom floor. Who was trying to get into the studio at this late hour?

She grabbed a baseball bat and approached the door. She came to a dead halt when she saw who stood outside the door.

Logan.

~*~

Logan stood outside of Michelle's studio entrance with a sheepish grin. He hoped that Michelle was happy to see him, but the smile faded when he noticed the green look on her face. "Michelle, are you okay? Let me in, please."

She didn't move. Her bottom lip quivered, and his heart went out to her. He placed his hands on the glass and yelled. "Open the door. I'm concerned about you." The way she was gazing at him hurt his heart and stirred his soul. *Please God, let her open the door and give me another chance.*

The sound of the door unlocking motivated him. He pushed it open and entered the studio. Michelle didn't move. She clenched the baseball bat in her hands. Her eyes were puffy. He reached out to touch her arm, but she stepped back.

"Why are you here?"

Because I love you. He treaded carefully. "I wanted to talk."

"About what?"

"Us."

"There is no us. I think you and your fiancée know that."

Logan frowned. What was she talking about? "I don't have a fiancée."

Her entire body shook. A sob broke through. Logan moved to take her into his arms and comfort her, but she pushed him away. "Don't touch me."

He respected her wishes and stepped back.

When Michelle's gaze met his again, her eyes were cold. She spoke slowly and with an even tone. "You need to leave."

"But, I…we need talk. Please."

She raised her voice, which trembled. "I said leave!"

Her sharp tone pierced him. He gulped and turned away then glanced back as he placed his hand on the door. She glanced away. He wanted to work things out, but now was not the time. Once he stepped outside, the lock clicked behind him. He turned around, but she'd already disappeared.

Logan's hands quivered. He retrieved his cell phone as he walked to his car. What was Michelle talking about him having a fiancée? He'd just started dating London again but had decided to break up with her. He'd called her to arrange a meeting in public where he would gently but firmly tell her it was over. However, she hadn't answered.

He reached his car and slipped into the driver's

seat. He'd just logged into Facebook where he saw that London had tagged him in a photo with a very bold caption. "We're getting married!" Logan's blood boiled.

Cameron was right. London was no good. His heart twisted. This must be what Michelle saw, and it would explain why she didn't want to talk to him.

He longed to take her in his arms and soothe her pain with the truth. He loved her not London. He wanted to be with Michelle. But now was not the time to have that conversation.

He tossed his cell phone to the empty passenger seat and shifted his car into drive. He may not be able to talk to Michelle right now, but he certainly could go to London's hotel and end their relationship tonight.

Chapter 19

Logan knocked on the door to London's hotel room and waited. It wasn't that late. She should still be up. After another knock, the door opened to reveal London dressed in her bathrobe. She yawned then smiled. "Good evening, love. What brings you to my room?"

"We need to talk."

"Sure. Come in." She gestured for him to enter.

He stepped inside, and London shut the door. "Can I get you anything to drink? I can call room service."

"No. This will be straight to the point."

She folded her arms and frowned. "Okay."

"Why did you do it?"

"Do what?"

Logan held out his phone fixed on her Facebook post with the false engagement news.

A rose hue colored London's cheeks, and she peered at Logan through her lashes. "Well, we are headed to the altar, aren't we?"

Logan finger-combed his hair. "No, we're not."

London furrowed her brow. "But I thought—"

"That's the problem. You think too much. You thought you could waltz back into my life and pick up where we left off. You thought that just because I agreed to give you another chance, we were going to get married. You hurt someone I love. Michelle doesn't deserve this."

London narrowed her eyes. "Someone you love? Michelle? Who is she?"

Heat rose from Logan's neck to his face.

"Sh-sh-she... It's none of your business."

"Is this about the girl from the café? The black girl sitting with her computer by the smoothie machine?"

"Why?"

"I saw the way you looked at her then rushed me out. Were you dating her?"

"Yes. We were dating."

London harrumphed.

"What?"

"I didn't know you were into black girls."

Logan fumed. "I didn't know you would ever say something like that." London had changed beyond reconciliation. Her words reaffirmed his decision to let her go.

She unfolded her arms and stepped toward him. "Oh, honey. Why would you want her when you could have me?" She reached out to touch his face. He blocked her hand and stepped back. The glint of a diamond ring—his engagement ring—caught his eye. He narrowed his eyes and held out his hand. "Give it back."

"Give what back?"

"The engagement ring. We're over, for good."

London steeled. "No. I want to fight for us, remember? I believe we're meant to be."

"You're delusional. I said we're over. I'm done. I don't want you in my life as my wife, or quite frankly, even as a friend."

Hurt flashed through London's eyes, and for a moment, Logan wondered if he went too far. But it was nowhere as far as London went. Yes, she was still beautiful, but her heart was ugly, and he was glad he realized it before it was too late.

London twisted the ring on her finger. Moments, later, she held it out to him. He took it from her grasp. Her hands trembled. She quickly folded her arms and stared at him.

"I wish you well, London. But please do not contact me anymore." He moved toward the door but stopped when she called out.

"You'll regret this. Letting me go is a mistake!"

~*~

Michelle rang the buzzer to Juliana's apartment. She tapped her feet. It was almost midnight, but she needed to talk to someone in person. Now if only Juliana would answer her door. She pressed the buzzer again then wrapped her arms around her waist, trying to steady her emotions by steadying her body.

A few seconds later, the door opened to reveal Juliana, dressed in her pajamas and yawning. Juliana's eyes widened.

Michelle's bottom lip quivered.

Juliana stepped aside. "Come in, amiga. What's

wrong?"

Michelle sunk into the plush white leather couch in Juliana's living room. She bent her legs beneath her and buried her head in her hands. She couldn't stop the waterfall that now cascaded down her cheeks.

"Oh, Juliana," Michelle cried. "How could I have been so stupid? Logan doesn't love me. He doesn't even like me anymore."

Juliana held Michelle and patted her upper back like a mother soothing a baby. She spoke in a hushed tone. "It's okay. You're not stupid. Maybe it's just a misunderstanding."

"You saw the picture. He's engaged."

"My pastor says you're single until you're married."

She pulled back and frowned. "What does that mean?"

"It means they're not legally bound to each other yet, so you still have a chance with Logan."

Michelle's shoulders shook. "No, I don't. He loves her. Not me."

"Are you sure?"

Michelle reached for the tissue box on the end table.

"Yes."

Juliana frowned. "How can you be so sure?"

"Lip lock and the bling of that ring don't lie."

"I think you and Logan need to talk."

Michelle wiped her eyes. "Why?"

"Because this could all be a misunderstanding, starting with what I saw in Annapolis. I've been thinking about it, and that woman he was with could have been his colleague."

Michelle sniffed. "They were acting too friendly to be just friends."

"I'm not so sure. I've seen Logan on TV. He's pretty friendly. He was probably just being himself but in a very platonic way."

"You saw Logan on TV?"

Juliana's eyebrows lifted. She opened her mouth then closed it before opening it again. "*Si*, amiga. He's the new evening anchorman for WJLA. You didn't know?"

"I haven't watched the news in months."

"Well that explains it."

Juliana paused. "So, what are you going to do? Because I think you should fight for your man."

"We never defined our relationship. He's not my man."

"Well then, I think you should talk first, clear up all of these misunderstandings, then make your relationship official."

"Why?"

Juliana grasped Michelle by the hands and gave a reassuring squeeze. "Because, amiga, I've never seen two people who are more meant to be than you and Logan. Call it best friend intuition. I've never seen you as happy and carefree as you are when you're talking about him. Well, not including tonight of course."

A small smile tugged at the corners of Michelle's lips. "You think so?"

Juliana leaned in. "I know so."

Michelle let out a laugh. It was a sound that she hadn't heard from herself in weeks. Maybe Juliana was right. The least she could do was let Logan explain himself. She would call him when she was ready.

Chapter 20

Michelle woke with a start. Loud, angry voices reached her ears. She rubbed her eyes and pulled herself off the cold, wooden floor she'd fallen on when the voices startled her from her midday nap. The voices escalated. She followed the sound to the front door. One of the voices—a strong baritone— she recognized. Marcel. Oh, no. Who was he talking to? She unlocked the door and swung it open.

Marcel stood in their parents' front yard in a shouting match with Dave and Diane, their new neighbors. She rushed outside and placed herself in between Marcel and the Rivers. "What's going on?"

Marcel pointed a finger at the Rivers. "They think I was trying to break into our home."

Dave spluttered. "Your home? This is your home?"

Marcel snorted. "What? You don't think a black family can afford to live in this upper-class neighborhood?"

"That is not what my husband meant," Diane

said.

Michelle's stomach tightened. She prayed for clarity and skill to be a good mediator. She turned to the Rivers. "I am so sorry about this misunderstanding."

Another snort from Marcel. "This ain't no misunderstanding, this is racial profiling."

Diane placed her hands on her hips. "We're not racists. Our grandbaby is black."

Marcel laughed. "Oh man, this is rich. You going to tell me that your best friend is black now too?"

Dave's eyes narrowed. "Now you listen here, son."

"Son? I am not your son."

Michelle took a deep breath and did something she rarely did. She shouted. "Everybody be quiet and listen!"

Dave and Diane stood with their mouths wide open. Marcel, well she would wait to look at him. She focused on the Rivers. "Dave and Diane, this is my brother Marcel. He moved out years ago, but sometimes he still visits us."

Dave folded his arms. "Really? Then tell us why he was snooping around your house."

Marcel leaned forward. "Because I lost my spare key. Not that it's any of your business."

Michelle turned to her brother. "Marcel, this is Dave Rivers and his wife Diane. They moved into our neighborhood a few weeks ago."

Marcel folded his arms. "I can't say it's nice to meet you."

Dave's face reddened. "Come on, Diane. We

don't need this bad reception." They started to walk away.

Marcel shouted. "Yeah? The feeling is mutual!"

"Do you have to be so rude?" Michelle's hands shook.

"Do you have to be so naive? They thought I was breaking into our parents' house just because I'm black in a rich neighborhood. If I were white, they wouldn't have thought anything of it."

"Yes, Marcel. That's a possibility, because that's the reality of the world that we live in, but Dave and Diane haven't seen you before. Most likely, they were concerned neighbors, that's all." Marcel's nostrils flared. "See? This is exactly why I don't want you dating that white boy. He's brainwashing you. Do you think you're going to escape racism just because you're with him now? You're still a black woman."

She forced herself to stand strong. "I'll have you know that Logan and I have not talked about race. We're not even talking right now."

"Good. It's in your best interest."

"I didn't say we're over. We're just not talking right now. Why do you have to be so angry? Logan's done nothing wrong to me or you."

"Yet. He hasn't done anything wrong to me or you yet. They cannot be trusted. Don't you remember the incident?"

Michelle's eyes clouded. She did remember the incident involving cops mistreating her brother and dad while Michelle and her Mom sat in their family BMW praying for God to intervene. The police had pulled them over. Dad was driving. They ordered

Marcel and Dad out of the car and pushed them to the ground. They interrogated them, claiming they were trying to cause trouble by driving slowly through a rich neighborhood. Only it was their neighborhood because they'd just moved in and wanted to take in the beautiful scenery of their new home.

The incident had added fuel to the fire that Marcel was already facing as a black man, and he'd never forgotten it. But that was two decades ago. Michelle and their parents did their best to forgive, release the injustices to God, and move on. But it was hard to forget when situations still arose in the news showing injustice against people of color.

She took a deep breath. "I cannot deny it was a traumatic experience for all of us. But you can't continue thinking that all white people can't be trusted. It's not fair."

"Fair? And mistreatment of black people in this world is fair?"

"No, it's not. But remember, earth is not our home. We need to keep our focus on Jesus."

Marcel slapped his thighs. He then took a deep breath. "It's great that you're trying to forgive, forget, and not hate anyone. You should win the Nobel Peace Prize. But I cannot forget how our people still deal with injustice everywhere we go. It doesn't happen every day, but the threat of being judged negatively and mistreated is always there. Just like today with your new white neighbors assuming the worst."

Michelle bit her lip. "I know."

For a moment, Marcel stared at her. "I'm here to

pick up a box containing a surprise for Mercedes. Mom said she left it on the kitchen table."

Marcel walked into the house. She peered over her shoulder. Dave and Diane had long been gone. She was grateful that they didn't call the cops and shivered as she thought of what could have happened if the police had been involved.

Lord, when will all the hate in this world come to an end? There's so much pain, and as much as I hate to admit it, I've seen the hate our people have to deal with. I can see why Marcel is so mad. But Lord, please touch his heart, heal his hurt, and help him give Logan and other good people like him a chance.

~*~

Michelle sat in front of her TV. Her parents had gone to bed early. She thanked God for the calmer atmosphere tonight compared to this afternoon. She curled up on the couch, pointed her remote control at the TV, flipped through the channels, and stopped on WJLA. The evening newscast was starting in a few minutes, and she was finally strong enough to see Logan again. Maybe not in person but watching him anchor the evening newscast was a start. She reached for her cup of peppermint tea on the end table.

She tightened her grasp on her mug when Logan's face appeared on the screen, and her heart melted when she heard his voice. He made it through the first segment without stuttering. She was so happy for him.

"Tonight, we're featuring a story that's close to my heart," Logan said. "Our special news segment focuses on an issue that affects many school-age children. Tonight, we're highlighting the journey of a brave and special boy, Charlie. He's your average preteen boy who loves sports and interacting with his friends, but he stutters.

"His speech impediment made him the victim of bullies, but he chose to tackle it head on. Charlie challenged his oppressors by starting a club for kids who are bullied, and the members of that club are gaining respect from their peers as they teach them empathy. They're also gaining ground in their learning community. The teachers at Charlie's school are actively involved in the campaign to combat this dangerous situation in schools across America, and it's not only creating empathy. It's raising awareness. This story is close to my heart because I too struggle with stuttering."

Michelle placed her cup down and leaned forward.

"I had people who believed in me and helped me survive my struggle. The man who gave me this job connected me with Sally Bridges who helped groom me. Thanks to Sally and other supporters like my mom, who is a speech therapist, I sit here every evening, delivering what I hope are flawless newscasts to you, stutter-free."

She missed Logan.

Juliana was right. Michelle and Logan needed to talk. Before she could dial, her phone rang. "Hey, Jules."

"Amiga, did you see Logan on TV tonight?"

"Yes."

"What do you think?"

I think I love him. "It was perfect. He's perfect."

"Did you see her?"

"Who?"

"Sally Bridges. The lady he said helped him to prepare for his job on TV. Oh Michelle, that's the woman I saw him with in Annapolis. She's not his girlfriend, and they're not dating. They were simply working together. I am so sorry for causing you to doubt Logan's love for you."

Michelle's heart rate kicked up. He hadn't been with her? "It's water under the bridge, Jules. It's my fault too. I should have talked to him about her instead of assuming."

"Like you said, it's water under the bridge. Now go call your man."

Michelle giggled. "Yes, ma'am."

As Michelle ended the call with Juliana, the image of Logan kissing the pretty blonde resurfaced. Her heart sank. She'd be devastated if he married someone else. They had something special together before that fiancée, and Michelle needed to know if they could work things out. She took a deep breath and dialed.

~*~

Logan did burpees. Not his most favorite exercise, but it was the most effective after planks. Being a TV personality meant he had to look his best, and while he wasn't overweight, he wanted to stay toned. He was grateful his parents allowed him to work out in their home gym.

His cell phone rang. He reached for it without looking at the caller ID. "Hello?"

"Hey, Logan."

He recognized the voice immediately, even after not hearing it for months. His hands sweated. What did it mean that she was calling him?

"It's Michelle."

"I know. Hey."

She took a deep breath. "I'm sorry."

Logan hoisted a heavy weight and laid it on a bench. "For what?"

"For pushing you away."

"It's okay. But I would like an explanation for why you stopped talking to me."

"Yes. I want to discuss that. Can we meet up?"

"Sure. What time works for you?"

"Maybe tomorrow for lunch?"

"Where do you want to eat?"

"My studio. It'll be closed. I'll bring take out, and we can eat it in my office."

"Sounds great."

"What would you like?"

"You choose. You've got great taste."

Was it his imagination or did a mild laugh escape Michelle? He smiled. "I look forward to seeing you."

"I look forward to seeing you tomorrow too."

They said their goodbyes. Suddenly, he felt like doing one hundred burpees. Did their relationship have a chance? Tomorrow, he would find out. But what if Michelle didn't want to resume their relationship? Would he settle for being a friend? He couldn't think the worst. He picked up the weight and prayed for the best.

Chapter 21

London stepped out of her rental car. She smoothed her figure-fitting emerald-green dress. She adjusted her sunglasses and reached for her purse before shutting her car door. Her only regret was wearing high heels. She didn't anticipate having to walk on cobblestone or a boardwalk which is what she had to do as she walked from the parking lot to the quaint but impressive photo studio, Love in Pictures.

After Logan took back her engagement ring and told her to stay out of his life, her blood boiled. She thought of the last and only time that a man had broken her heart—her high school boyfriend who was her first love but broke up with her before prom, leaving her dateless and at home on a weekend. She never spent weekends alone. She was always in a relationship. That breakup threw her, but she bounced back, meeting a new boyfriend her freshman year of college and then shortly after college, she met Logan. He was everything she wanted...until now.

Now she just wanted to get even. She may not be able to reach Logan directly anymore, but she wasn't leaving for Paris tonight without having a word with the woman who took him from her. Moments later, she stood outside the studio.

She tried to ignore the fact that the exterior was beautiful with a sleek, modern design. The business name, Love in Pictures, was in bold, fancy but easy-to-read lettering that was perfectly accented with a feminine touch.

London peered through the window. The studio's interior was warm and welcoming with pastel color furniture and light that was bright enough to fill the room and take good pictures, but soft enough to not blind the eyes. It looked even better than the picture she saw online when she'd hunted Michelle down.

London inhaled sharply. So, what if this Michelle Hadley had a beautiful workplace, one that she owned? London was a famous model with a growing fan base. She was prettier than Michelle, too, and worthier of Logan's heart. After steeling herself for this planned confrontation, London opened the front door and stepped inside. She perched her sunglasses on top of her head and approached the receptionist desk. "Michelle Hadley, please."

The receptionist looked awed and astonished. London assumed it was because of her beauty and confidence.

"Excuse me?"

London glared down at the petite woman behind

the desk. "I need to talk with Michelle Hadley. This is her studio, is it not?"

Before the receptionist could answer, another woman spoke in a soft, professional tone. "I am Michelle Hadley, and this is my studio. How may I help you?"

London smiled. She turned to face the woman Logan chose over her. She held out her hand. "My name is London. Can we talk in private?" Michelle gave a firm handshake but a timid smile. "Sure. But may I ask what this is in regard to?"

"My fiancé. We'd like for you to be our wedding photographer."

Michelle smiled. "Oh, then you need a consultation. We're closing for lunch break in ten minutes. Can we schedule a time for next week?"

London stood strong. "We need to talk now. I fly out to Paris tonight."

"Oh. Okay. My consultations take more than ten minutes to be effective. Let me give you my business card."

London couldn't wait any longer. She decided to do this now. She retrieved her phone from her purse, unlocked it, and thrust it in Michelle's face. "This is my fiancé. Isn't he a good-looking man?"

Michelle blanched. She took a step back and studied London. Her eyes widened, and London smiled smugly. She hoped Michelle was recognizing her as the woman Logan loved. So what if his love for her faded years ago? It could happen again. Logan belonged to her, not Michelle.

"You're, you're…"

The receptionist spoke up. "Miche? Is

everything okay?"

Before Michelle could respond, the door chime sounded. Michelle looked over London's shoulder, and her eyes welled with tears. London turned around to see who walked in. She faced Logan. His eyes were cold, and he addressed her in a carefully measured voice. "London? Why are you here?"

London stepped toward him to give him a kiss but he stepped aside. She steeled. "I thought I'd give your fake girlfriend a sayonara before I hopped on my plane to Paris, love."

London heard the sound of footfalls. She didn't have to turn around to figure out Michelle was exiting the scene. Good. She needed to leave. London belonged in Logan's arms, not Michelle. She frowned as she watched Logan look over her shoulder and call out to Michelle. "Michelle, wait! Please."

London heard a door shut. She smiled. This was perfect. She made eye contact with Logan. Sure, he was mad now, but once he finally took her back, he'd be happy again. She was sure of it. She ignored the fact that Logan's fists were clenched. He looked at London intently. "Would you please step outside with me?"

She nodded and followed Logan. The scent of fresh water and crisp, cool air greeted them. She spoke first. "I told you that you were making a mistake. Leave her and come back to me."

He stood still. He paused before speaking. "You're out of your mind. I told you a few nights ago we are over and not to contact me. Why are you going after Michelle? She didn't do anything to you."

London stepped forward. She reached out to touch him, but he stepped to the side. Realizing that she was now reaching for air, she withdrew her hand and used it to clench her purse. "I'm here to win you back. She doesn't deserve you."

He folded his arms. "So, I assume you think that you do?"

"Of course. We were perfect together. We were going to get married, start a family, maybe even move to Paris, remember?"

Logan let out a low breath. "That was then, but this is now. Back then I didn't know you was well as I thought, but during these last two weeks, I see the real you clearly, and I don't like it."

London was appalled. "The real me?"

"Yes. I'm going to tell you one last time. I have no interest in pursuing a relationship with you. Please leave for good and don't bother me or Michelle. Stay out of our lives. You don't belong here."

London clenched her fists and narrowed her eyes. "Fine. I don't need you. I cannot believe that I ever considered being your wife. Clearly, I deserve better."

Logan didn't say a word. His silence made her madder. She resisted the urge to pummel his chest with her fists. She inhaled sharply and turned away from him. As she walked to her car, she huffed, silently fuming. She didn't dare to turn around to steal a glance at his reaction. If her performance at Michelle's studio today worked, Michelle would never take him back.

Chapter 22

Logan rapped on the Michelle's office door. "Let me in, please. I can explain."

No response. Only muffled cries. His throat closed, and his chest tightened. Why did London have to mess with Michelle's mind? He prayed this last interaction with London was the final one and she would heed his words and stay out of his life.

The receptionist approached the door. "I'm going to lunch. Locking the studio behind me." She studied Logan. "You're going to have to leave."

The door opened, and Michelle stood there, hair disheveled, eyes red. She directed her attention at the receptionist. "Go ahead. I'll show him out."

The receptionist bit her bottom lip and walked away. He faced Michelle. "Hey, I'm sorry about today. I didn't know London was going to be here."

Michelle glared. "Really? So, this all just happened? Out of the blue?"

"Actually, it did. I broke up with her a few nights ago. We're history."

"You broke up with her?" Michelle stepped back. "So, you were dating her the same time you were dating me? Unbelievable." She wiped the tears from her eyes.

"I wasn't dating her when I was dating you. She just returned to town two weeks ago."

"So, you picked up right where you left off? And you gave her a ring a few days after being reunited?"

Logan sighed. This was going to take a lot of explaining. "Can we sit down?"

"I don't know if we can do anything together. Why are you here?"

"Because we agreed to do lunch today and talk things out, remember?"

Michelle glanced away then back at him. "Fine. Sit. Talk, then leave."

"Fair enough. But promise to hear me through before you throw me out."

She stepped aside so he could enter her office. They sat at a small conference table. Starting with how he and London met years ago, he explained everything to Michelle, including his surprise when she showed up at the news station while he was on air. "When I saw you with that Italian guy, I was jealous."

"Of what?"

"Him. He got what I thought I couldn't have. That stung."

"Like I misunderstood about the speech coach."

"Huh?"

She played with the pencil that had been sitting on the table. "Juliana spied the two of you one day seeming very chummy with each other. She snapped a picture, and I snapped to judgment. That's why I didn't call you. We didn't realize who that was until we saw your story on the news the other night."

"Guess I can't blame you when I did the same thing. Anyway, Cameron helped me see the light. I'm sorry to have put you through all that. Especially the scene with London. She was way out of line. If I'd only known she was going to show up here, I would have stopped her."

Michelle inhaled sharply. "And I'm sorry I misunderstood you about her. But when I saw the picture of you kissing and the engagement announcement, I...I just couldn't handle it, so I distanced myself from you."

He reached out, and she allowed him to touch her hands. "I know. But I never did reinstate my engagement with London. The photo was a lie. What you don't see is what happened later. She showed me her true colors. She's a horrible person, which is why I told her to leave."

Michelle's hands trembled. "What if she shows up again and, well, does something?"

"She won't."

Michelle furrowed her brow. "How can you be so sure?"

"She cares too much about her reputation with the public to ever do anything that would show her in a negative light or give her trouble. She was only trying to intimidate you. Don't fall for it."

Michelle pressed both sides of her temple. "I don't know. This is all so complicated."

"Let me uncomplicate it for you. I want you, Michelle, not London or any other woman in the world."

She peered at him through her lashes. "Why?"

Because you're everything to me. "Because I care about you, and I'd like to explore the concept of us."

A small smile tugged at the corner of her lips. "Us?"

"Yes, I'd love to make us an item. If you'll have me."

Michelle blushed, and his chest expanded. But then she sighed. "I don't know. I care about you, too, but all of this and with my brother. It's just putting me through an emotional wringer, and I'm not sure I can do this."

Logan frowned. "Your brother? What's he got to do with us?"

Michelle chortled. "Everything. He doesn't want me dating you."

"Why not?"

"Marcel, my brother, is not exactly your biggest fan."

Logan drew in a breath. "I don't understand. I haven't met the man. Why?"

She wrung her hands.

He sighed. "Just tell me. I can take it."

"Marcel doesn't like that I'm dating you because…"

"Because what?"

Michelle mumbled.

He leaned in. "What did you say?"

"Because you're white."

"What? What does that have to do with us?"

She glanced at the clock. "Do you mind if we get lunch and talk about this later? I need to return to work within the hour."

A million questions flew through Logan's mind. But he agreed. "Fair enough."

They walked to the restaurant in silence. He took the opportunity to pray. *Dear God, what is this? There's someone else who wants to tear us apart? London was enough. Please remove any more obstacles. I really care about Michelle. Please, don't let me lose her.*

"Do you like Mexican food?"

Michelle's words jolted Logan out of his silent talk with God as they reached Mariana's Mesa. "Sure."

Minutes later, they had their food and found an empty table. After a few spicy bites, Logan wiped his mouth. "So, about your brother. Why doesn't he want you dating a white guy?"

Michelle swallowed. "He's a great man, he really is, but he's experienced a lot of hate and been in situations where people discriminated against him just because he's black."

"Like with the cops?"

She tensed. "Among other things."

"So, what does this have to do with me and with us?" He scooped up some guacamole with a chip.

"It's complicated. Have you ever dated a woman of color before?"

"No."

She nodded and bit into her chicken taco.

"What about it?"

"You need to be prepared. It's going to be different."

"Different how?"

"Different like I think we'll find out if there is an us."

"What does that mean?"

"People can be prejudiced. Even in this day and age, not everyone likes to see an interracial relationship."

Michelle's words punched him in the gut. He pushed his plate aside and stared at the one woman he loved like no other. "Why does it matter? I care about you and your happiness. I want to be there for you. Why should I care about what ignorant people say?"

"That's sweet. I agree, but it's not the reality of the world we live in."

The food churned in his stomach. "Then what are you saying? You don't want to do this?"

Michelle reached out and took Logan's hands into hers. "I want us to work, I really do. You need to understand this isn't going to be easy."

"I can see this is important to you, and I don't want anything else to get in the way of us moving forward. I'd like to have a conversation with your brother, man-to-man."

She raised her eyebrows. "You want to talk to him? When?"

"Maybe this weekend?"

"Okay, if you're sure about this."

"Of course I am." What could go wrong?

Michelle swallowed her food. "Okay. I'll call you with the logistics."

She gulped the remainder of her drink and glanced at her watch. "I've got to get back to the studio. Lunch break is over."

Logan stood. "I'll walk you back."

He reached the door first and held it open for her. As they exited the building, he paused and gently took Michelle into his arms. "We're going to be okay. I'm willing to wait for you to figure things out and for the coast to be clear concerning your brother."

Michelle's eyes misted. He longed to kiss her concerns into oblivion, but he respected her wishes to take things slow. So instead, he stroked her hair. His heart swelled with love for her, but he knew now was not the time to talk. He drew her into a hug. "Be safe. We'll talk tomorrow."

He let her go and walked away. Hopefully it wouldn't take her too long to figure out what she wanted.

Chapter 23

Cameron bounced the basketball back and forth between his legs. He fixed his gaze on the hoop, lifted his heels and arms. Seconds later, the swoosh confirmed Cameron made yet another perfect shot. He turned around, grinned at Logan, and bounced the ball to him. "Beat that."

Normally, he could beat Cameron, if only by one point. But today, he wasn't into the competition. His upcoming conversation with Marcel distracted him.

Cameron slapped him on the back. "What's up, man? You okay?"

Logan shook his head. "No. I have to talk to Michelle's brother later this afternoon."

Cameron quirked his eyebrow. "Your Michelle? You're back together?"

"Not yet, but if tonight goes well, then yes."

Cameron tossed the basketball between his hands. "What's happening tonight?"

"I'm meeting her brother."

"Okay. So, what's the problem?"

"Her brother doesn't want me dating her."

Cameron's face blanked. "What? Why not?"

"Because I'm white."

Cameron covered his mouth.

Was he laughing? "It's not funny, man. Can you help me understand?"

Cameron stepped back. "What? You want me to give you the black perspective now?"

"No. Well, maybe. I need to know how I can impress her brother and convince him I'm good for her."

Cameron eyed Logan then nodded. "Okay man, here's what you need to do. First, be yourself. Once Michelle's brother sees past your skin color, he might become more agreeable. He probably has experienced some prejudice and hate, and that's why he's so defensive. It's not easy being a black man in America."

"I don't understand."

"Exactly."

"Exactly what?"

"There's a lot that you're just not going to understand. There's a certain level of privilege you enjoy as a white American, even if you're unaware. My advice is you need to listen and try to sympathize even if you can't empathize. Try not to discredit his feelings and experiences because they may seem strange to you."

Logan nodded. This was a lot to take in.

"Michelle sounds like a strong woman. So be careful not to mess with her emotions, or she may reject you for good. This whole interracial dating experience may be new to her, and clearly, it's new to you. You both need to tread carefully."

Logan exhaled.

"It's a lot to think about, but I think that things between you and Michelle will work out because from what you tell me, she made you believe in love again." Cameron thrust the basketball into Logan's chest. "So, don't mess it up."

Logan held the ball underneath his right arm. "Thanks, man. But what should I say to Michelle's brother?"

"I told you. Listen. Talk less. And pray about it before you talk to him. Now come on, let's shoot some hoops. It will relieve your stress."

Logan bounced the basketball. "You ready to get beat?"

Cameron harrumphed. "Not today, man. I'm going to win by a landslide."

"We'll see about that." Logan bounced the ball toward the hoop and pushed past Cameron's defense. As he made perfect shot after perfect shot, he prayed his meeting with Marcel would go as well.

~*~

Logan sipped from the tall glass of water as he sat at the bar of an Irish restaurant. He glanced over to Michelle a few feet away as she scrolled through her phone. She tapped her feet. Given their situation tonight, she probably wasn't moving to the music.

He refocused his attention on his half-empty glass of water and pushed it to the side before picking up his phone. Before he could type anything, it beeped with a text alert from Michelle.

Michelle: *Here he comes. Act natural. Let me butter him up, then I'll send you a text. That will be your signal to approach our table.*

Logan cast a glance in Michelle's direction. She stood and greeted a tall black man with the strong, agile build of an athlete. He gave her a bear hug and said something. They both pulled back and laughed. Their smiles were identical. They sat across from each other at the table. A few minutes later, his phone beeped. Michelle just sent his cue.

Please God, help me.

He slid off his tall bar stool and strolled to them. As he approached, Marcel glanced up, and he frowned.

Michelle greeted Logan with a brave smile. "Hey." She gestured to the empty chair. "Have a seat."

Logan sat and turned to Marcel. He smiled and extended his right hand. "So nice to meet you. Michelle has told me—"

Anger flashed through Marcel's coffee-brown eyes. He ignored Logan's extended hand and fixed his gaze on Michelle. "What's he doing here?"

Her lips quivered. "I'd like for you to meet my friend, Logan." She turned to Logan. "And Logan, I'd like for you to meet my brother, Marcel."

Marcel pushed his chair back, but Michelle reached across the table and stilled him with the touch of her hand. "Please, just hear him out. For me?"

Marcel clenched his fists then inhaled. He returned to his seat and glared at Logan. "You have five minutes."

Logan chuckled. "Five minutes is all I need."

Michelle grabbed her purse. "I'm going to freshen up. Why don't you two talk?"

Logan cleared his throat. "Nice to meet you."

Marcel narrowed his eyes. "I cannot say the same."

Remember to listen. Cameron's advice echoed in Logan's head. "Michelle is a great girl. I really care about her. She's special, and I'd like your blessing on our relationship."

"I'm her brother not her father. Why do you need my blessing?"

Logan hadn't thought of that. Was it possible Michelle's parents were more easygoing? He made a mental note to ask Michelle. "Yes, well, I'd like the whole family's blessing."

Marcel's focus became intent. "Why do you want to date my sister?"

Logan refused to tap his foot to the fast beat of his heart. He forced himself to speak. "B-b-because..." *Please God, not now.*

For a moment, a combination of concern and understanding flashed through Marcel's eyes. Was this Logan's window? "Please excuse me. I have a problem with stuttering."

Marcel didn't say a word. Logan cleared his throat.

"I r-r-really like your sister. She's a wonderful woman, and it's an honor to have her in my life. I hope you can respect our mutual attraction and not interfere."

Marcel snorted. "You don't get it, do you?"

"Get what?"

"Whatever this thing you have going on with my sister, it's not going to last. There's too much hate in this world."

"What do you mean?"

"Do you really think you can date a black woman without interference from ignorant people?"

Was Marcel calling himself ignorant?

Logan stuttered. "I…I…uhh."

"Don't tell me Michelle is the first woman of color you've dated, is she?"

All Logan could do was nod.

"Great. Just great."

Logan's Irish blood heated. But he chose his words with care. "I don't understand why you hate me. You don't even know me."

Marcel leaned in and spoke with measured words. "And I don't understand why your people hate me without even knowing me."

"What?"

Marcel leaned back. "Exactly. You have no clue what you're getting into, do you?"

Clenching his fists, Logan stood. "Apparently not."

Before he could leave, Michelle rushed to the table. "Hey guys. How'd your talk go?"

Marcel came to his feet. "I'll catch you later, Miche."

Michelle's eyes widened. "Why? Where are you going?"

Her brother waved as he walked away.

"Logan, what's wrong? What happened?" Her honey-brown eyes shimmered.

He loved this woman, but he couldn't tolerate

her brother, and after their failed intervention, he needed to clear his head. "I'll call you later." He strode toward the exit. Hopefully the silence would help him hear God, because only God could help him now.

Chapter 24

"Hey sis!"

Michelle hugged her sister-in-law Mercedes then pulled back and looked around. "Is Marcel here?"

Mercedes nodded. "He's in his man cave and not in the best mood. He came home like that. Do you know why?"

"Yes. May I see him?"

"Go ahead. I was just making dinner. Want to join us?"

The mouthwatering scent of chicken enchiladas wafted under Michelle's nose. She'd love to stay, but though she was always invited in their home, Marcel might want his space tonight. "I'm not sure yet. Let me talk to Marcel first."

Mercedes shut her front door and locked it. "Sure. You know the way."

Michelle wandered through the contemporary kitchen with Spanish influences. Hexagonal terracotta tiles lined the floor, the walls were a beautiful cream color, and the kitchen cabinets were a dark walnut. With Mercedes's flair for decorating, every room was warm and welcoming.

She descended the basement stairs and tiptoed to Marcel's man cave. She paused at the door and closed her eyes. *Dear Lord, please help us.* She knocked.

"Babe, I need to be left alone."

Michelle swallowed. "It's not Mercedes. It's Michelle."

Silence. Michelle knocked again. More silence. Michelle twisted the knob and cracked the door.

"Marcel?"

Her brother sat in his easy chair with his back to her, facing the television but staring at a black screen. She tiptoed around his chair and plopped on the beanbag across from him, crossing her legs and sitting up straight.

Marcel's gaze trailed from the TV screen to Michelle. "Why are you here?"

"To make things right with the brother who means the world to me."

Marcel scoffed. "Really? Then how do you explain that ambush at the restaurant?"

Michelle paused. "It wasn't an ambush. All I wanted was an opportunity for you and Logan to talk and get to know each other. You both matter so much to me. I want us all to get along."

Marcel raised an eyebrow. "Why? Are you thinking of marrying that man?"

Michelle's heart flip flopped. She didn't know if he'd propose to her someday. After all, they were not even an official couple yet. But she wouldn't dash that dream. Logan was like no other man she knew. He made her so happy, made her feel loved and secure. But she wasn't about to go there with Marcel.

She chose her words with care. "I can't say yes or no to that question. But I can say that everyone deserves the right to be treated with respect and agape love, even if they look different from you."

Marcel raised both eyebrows. "You think I don't know that? I'm a Christian too. Just like you. Only I'm not as naive."

Marcel's words stung, but Michelle persevered. "Why do you think I'm naive?"

Marcel sat up straight and leaned forward. "Really, Miche? Do you really think people are going to accept you when you're with Logan? Do you really think people are going to root for your relationship?"

"I don't care what other people think. I care about Logan, and I care about my family. If only you would try to get to know him, I'm sure—"

"You're sure about what? That we'll all get together and sing a song about unity? The real world doesn't work like that. Remember the hate I faced when I was dating Mercedes? And she's Latina."

"Yes. I do remember. But you two love each other and are the perfect match. Why can't you see that possibility with me and Logan?"

"We're both minorities and know what it's like to be scared of white cops who racially profile people of color."

"But not all white cops are bad."

"True, but the one who pulled me over last year was bad. He made me get out of the car and pushed me to the ground all because he didn't like the tone of my voice. I had to appease him and calm him down, truly pacify him to avoid going to jail for what he considered a minor offense. It was the most humiliating moment of my life. He let me go with a speeding ticket and an uncalled-for jeer. I was so shaken I could barely drive home."

Michelle's heart ached for her brother. "I'm sorry you had a bad experience, and I'm not so naive that I don't think ignorant people won't hate me and Logan. But I'm prepared to ignore those kinds of comments and stares because he's a great guy and he cares about me and I care about him. I want to see where this goes."

Marcel sat back and let out a heavy sigh. "Do what you want. You're a grown woman. But don't expect me to pick up the pieces when he breaks your heart."

Michelle fought back tears. "Why do you think he will break my heart?"

For a moment, concern flashed through Marcel's eyes. "I'll try to be nice, because you're my sister and I love you. But because of what I've experienced over the years, I cannot agree with your new relationship with Logan. Do Mom and Dad know about him?"

"Yes. I tell Mom everything, and she tells Dad everything. You know that."

He didn't speak for a moment. When he did, his voice was measured. "Just be careful, Miche. I don't want to see you get hurt."

"I understand your concerns. But would you please just try to give Logan a chance? He respects you and wants to be on your good side."

Marcel picked up his remote control and turned on the TV.

She bit her bottom lip. "I'm leaving now."

Silence.

She wiped a tear that escaped from her eyes and quietly left. At the top of the stairs, she almost collided with Mercedes who was taking dinner out of the oven. She reached out to prevent Mercedes from fumbling with the food. "Sorry, sis. Are you okay?"

Mercedes let out a light-hearted laugh. "Yes, me and my food survived." She placed the casserole dish on a cooling rack on the island counter. "Is everything okay? What happened?"

Michelle's bottom lip trembled. Mercedes embraced her in a bear hug as her tears fell. "Marcel doesn't like my boyfriend."

Mercedes pulled away. "You got a new boyfriend?"

Michelle wiped her tears. "Yes, well, no. I want to take it slow. We haven't defined our relationship yet."

"Well, girl, tell me the story!"

A laugh escaped Michelle.

"Dinner's still cooking. Come sit with me in the kitchen, and we'll talk."

They took seats across from each other at the table, and Michelle told Mercedes everything.

Mercedes's mouth was agape. "What? Girl, I need to meet this man."

Michelle cast her gaze downward. "Marcel wouldn't like that."

Mercedes touched Michelle's hands. "Don't worry. I'll talk to my husband. I'm sure I can help him understand why you want to be with Logan. And from the sound of it, this may be his future brother-in-law. So, I'll make sure he gives Logan a fair chance. Brothers got to get along even if they look different." Mercedes gave Michelle's hands a reassuring squeeze.

Relief washed over her. If anyone could convince Marcel to give Logan a fair chance and get along with him, it was Mercedes. She got up and gave Mercedes a hug. "Thanks, sis."

Mercedes returned the hug. "You're welcome, girl."

"Are you staying for dinner? I fixed Marcel's favorite meal."

At the savory scent of chicken enchiladas, green beans, and caramel-topped flan, Michelle's mouth watered. But she declined the dinner invitation.

"Are you sure?"

Michelle nodded.

"Okay. Maybe next time then. Let me walk you out."

Michelle followed Mercedes to her front door. She gave her one more hug before leaving. "Thanks, sis. I love you."

"Love you too, sis. Marcel loves you too. He just needs time to heal and see Logan isn't like the others."

Michelle was silent. Hopefully, Mercedes was right. Once inside her car, Michelle rested against the steering wheel. *Please God, soften Marcel's heart and make a way for him to accept my relationship with Logan. We need You, Lord.*

Chapter 25

Logan stood outside of Michelle's studio with a bouquet of multicolor roses. Since he didn't know her favorite flower color, he chose all the colors in this special arrangement. He decided to surprise Michelle at work and treat her to lunch, but the closed sign was already on the door.

He called her. A few rings later, she answered.

"Hello?"

"Hey, Michelle. It's me."

"I know. How are you?"

"Great. I'm actually standing outside of your studio. Are you in there?"

"Yes. Hold on."

Logan pressed the end button on his phone and slipped it into his pocket. He prayed for his talk with Michelle about Marcel to go well but figured it would be better if he wooed her with roses and fed her first.

Moments later, Michelle approached dressed in a pink sundress and matching sandals, sweet and delicate like the flowers he held. She opened the door, and he grinned. "Hey, beautiful."

"Hey."

He stepped in and presented her with the flowers. She accepted with a smile. "Thanks. This is sweet and very unique. I love the colors."

Logan chuckled. "I didn't know your favorite."

Michelle's eyes sparkled. "So, you bought them all?"

Logan gave a sheepish grin. Michelle laughed, and his heart warmed.

"My favorite flower color is anything you are inspired to buy for me. So, this is perfect."

He drew her into an embrace. "Good to know." He kissed her forehead, and for a moment, they shared a silent embrace. His heart swelled with love for this woman. He gazed into her eyes. "Can I treat you to lunch?"

Michelle glanced at the clock. "I do have the full hour. So sure, why not?"

"Where would you like to go?"

"Mariana's Mesa is really good, and they have a nice patio. I'd like to eat outside. The weather's perfect today. Just let me grab my purse and keys."

Logan allowed her to retrieve her items, and they exited her studio. After she locked the door, they strolled side by side down the street to Mariana's Mesa. Minutes later, they'd ordered their food and waited for their meal at a table on the patio that overlooked the water. Seagulls squawked, nearby children laughed, and adults conversed in varied tones of voice.

Michelle's gaze was fixed on the water. "I love

living and working in Annapolis."

"Yeah. Me too."

Michelle focused on Logan. "I almost don't want to talk about it."

"About what?"

"Your meeting with Marcel. What went wrong?"

This conversation was inevitable. So, he manned up. "He's not too happy about us becoming a couple."

"I know."

"But he didn't let me explain myself. He has this preconceived notion about me, like I'm a bad guy, and I'm not."

"I know."

"Then what can we do about this? I really like you."

Michelle reached and grasped him by the hand. She spoke softly. "I really like you too."

For a moment, they stared into each other's eyes. The waitress arrived with their order of food and placed it on the table, interrupting their moment. She smiled. "Enjoy!"

As their waitress walked away, Michelle withdrew her hands and drizzled her bean taco with mango salsa. She bit into it. "Mmm. So good."

Logan chomped on his steak quesadilla, and for a few minutes, they concentrated on their food. Logan broke the silence. "What can I do to convince your brother that I'm worth your time?"

Michelle wiped a string of cheese from the corner of her mouth. "I think Mercedes is working on that."

"Who's Mercedes?"

"My sister-in-law."

"Oh. She's a persuasive person?"

"Very."

A weight lifted from his chest. "Good. But what can I do in the meanwhile?"

A smile tugged at the corners of Michelle's lips.

"What?"

"Just be your loveable self."

"You think I'm loveable?"

"Completely."

He picked up another piece of his steak taco and chewed it. "I never knew people had to deal with these issues."

"Welcome to my world. It's not always on the forefront of my mind, but as a person of color, race-related issues are part of my reality."

Logan's shoulders sank. "I'm sorry you've had to deal with this."

Michelle reached for her tall glass of strawberry lemonade. "I've had to deal with it at work too."

"At your studio?"

She shook her head. "No. I have a great team of employees who are diverse and get along well with each other. But I've had to fight to get my clients of color on the covers of mainstream wedding magazines."

Logan frowned. "Why?"

"I think it's partly because of the European beauty standard. The people who make the final decisions about covers probably think only white women who mirror that standard are worthy, because rarely do they choose women of color to grace those magazines. Next time you're in a grocery store or a bookstore, look at the wedding magazines and tell me what you see. Mostly only white brides, and even then, it's usually blondes and brunettes."

"Wow. I never noticed."

"Most people who aren't of color don't. It's like we live in another society where we're always on the outside looking in."

Logan's heart ached. "Miche, I'm so sorry."

"I appreciate your trying to understand."

"For the record, my family would love to meet you."

Michelle's eyes sparkled. "Really?"

"My mom wants to meet the first girl I cooked dinner for on my boat."

Michelle quirked an eyebrow. "You never brought your dates to your boat?"

Logan shook his head and chewed his food.

"Wow. I must be pretty special then, eh?"

"Very."

Michelle leaned forward. "I'd love to meet your parents."

"Great. It's a date. I'll call you with the logistics."

Michelle glanced at her watch. "I need to return to the studio in ten minutes. Are you ready to go?"

Logan nodded and placed the money for the lunch on the table.

She smiled. "Are you going to pay for every meal we eat together?"

"Yes, because I'm a good boyfriend."

"You're going to be a broke boyfriend."

"As long as you're my girlfriend, I can live with being broke."

Michelle blushed. "Does this mean that we're an official couple?"

"Only if you like the idea of us."

Michelle leaned into his side. "I love the idea of us."

"Good, because I do too." He kissed her temple. His parents would welcome her with open arms even though he hadn't mentioned her race. Surely, they wouldn't have a problem with Michelle. But then again, prior to falling for Michelle, he never knew anyone would have a problem with a woman based solely on her skin color. He prayed his parents would be accepting of her.

Chapter 26

Logan rang the doorbell to his parents' house. They weren't going to like the fact that he forgot his spare keys. Again.

Thankfully, they always welcomed him to his childhood home with open arms, making visiting them worth the hour drive. Their home, in a beautiful neighborhood in Potomac, was full of unconditional love and good memories. Today, he wanted to catch up with Mom and arrange a date to bring Michelle to dinner.

Before he could ring the bell again, Isabella, his parents' maid, opened the door with a bright smile. "*Señor* Logan! *Bienvenido*!"

Logan hugged Isabella. "Thanks. Good to see you." He peered over her shoulder. "Are my parents home?"

"*Sí. Tu madre y tu padre están aquí.*"

"Good. I'm glad that they're here." Isabella and his nanny Florence taught him Spanish as a child. He heard and spoke it fluently but often answered in

English. "Where are they?"

"*En la cocina.*"

Logan nodded. In the kitchen. He made his way through the foyer and dining area into the elaborate, Texan-country style kitchen. His mother stood over the stove, arms folded, and tapped her foot as she stared at the kettle. The fire was on full blaze beneath the kettle, and the scent of peppermint filled the air. A chuckle escaped Logan. His mother never did like to wait for her tea to be ready.

She gazed at him. Her blue eyes sparkled, and her countenance glowed like a bright light. She rushed into his arms. "Hi, honey! Welcome home."

Caught off guard by her greeting, he hugged her back before pulling away. "Hey, Mom."

"We haven't seen you in four weeks. Don't do that. You're our only child. We need to see you at least once a week."

"I'm sorry. I'll try to keep our weekly family dinner dates."

"You'd better. Your father and I are always happy to have you home."

Logan glanced around. "Where is Dad?"

The kettle whistled, and Mom spun on her heel to tend to it. Steam rose from the mug that she covered with a plate to allow the tea to steep. "He's working late in the office. He should be home before midnight."

"Ah, the life of an attorney."

"That's why you shouldn't miss our Sunday dinners. Makes him stop working for a while. Would you like a cup of tea?"

He finger-combed his hair. "No, but thanks."

His mother tilted her head. "What?"

He pulled out a chair at the kitchen table for Mom and then sat in the one next to it. "Can we sit?"

Mom frowned. She picked up her mug and positioned herself next to Logan. "What is it, honey?"

"I…I…uh… You know I met someone?"

Mom flashed a wide grin. "Yes. Michelle. The one you cooked dinner for on your boat."

"Yes. I… I..."

"You love her. I know."

Logan was floored. His mother was insightful, but this was too true to how he felt about Michelle. "How did you know?"

"A mother's intuition is a very good and accurate thing." She removed the plate from her tea and blew the steam away. "So, when do we get to meet her? Your father and I want to see this woman who inspires you."

"I'd like to bring her to dinner this Sunday."

Mom sipped her tea before responding. "Done. I'll have Mario fix enough for the four of us. Does she have any food allergies?"

Logan shook his head and fidgeted in his seat.

She placed her mug on the table. "I know that look. What are you not telling me?"

Logan exhaled. "She's… I… They… I don't know how to tell you this."

Mom leaned forward. "Just tell me."

"She's black."

Mom chuckled. "Well that's not the end of the world."

Logan let out a sigh of relief. "You mean it doesn't matter?"

Mom shrugged. "Why should it? You're my son, and you met a woman who makes you happy, and from what I can tell, she's good for you. I'd love to meet her."

He relaxed against the back of the chair. "Thanks."

"Why were you worried about telling me?"

Logan sighed. "There are people who have a problem with me dating a black woman, and I just don't get it. On top of that, she's told me about some of her negative experiences. But it's all new to me."

Mom nodded. "People are going to talk no matter what you do and who you're with. What matters is that you love her, and I do believe she loves you too. You both need to protect your relationship, trust God to strengthen your bond, and focus on each other, not the people in this world who want to tear you apart."

Logan soaked in his mother's words of wisdom. "You're right. But the other problem is that her brother doesn't want me to date her. He hates me."

"Hate is a strong word. Why do you think that?"

Logan deadpanned. "Because I'm white."

"It's not going to be easy, because I've seen how our society oppresses black people. He's probably just responding to his negative experiences. Don't take it too personally. Be your considerate, wonderful self, treat him kindly, and he'll come around eventually, especially when he sees how well you treat his sister."

"Really? You think so?"

"I believe so."

"I hope you're right."

"So, let's plan our dinner date with Michelle. What do you want Mario to cook?"

A familiar text message sound alerted Logan.

Michelle: *Hey, babe. What are you up to?*

He peered at Mom, who was sipping her tea again. "It's Michelle." He returned his attention to his phone.

Logan: *Here at my parents' house, talking dinner plans for us this Sunday. Are you free?*

Michelle: *Yes!*

Logan: *Great! So maybe chicken or steak?*

Michelle: *Would love that! Sounds good!*

Logan: *Thanks, babe. Let me finish visiting with Mom. Want to do dinner tonight?*

Michelle: *Can't. I have to work late. Maybe we can meet for lunch later on this week?*

Logan: *Deal.*

He silenced his phone. Mom had a knowing grin plastered on her face.

"What?"

"I cannot wait to meet Michelle. Never have I seen you this happy, not even with London."

Logan winced.

Mom reached out and touched his hand. "I'm sorry, honey. I'm just happy you found love again and even happier that this looks like the forever kind."

Logan sat back. "London was here. I spoke with her during that time I told you about when Michelle and I weren't talking."

"Really? What happened?"

Logan spent fifteen minutes telling his mom about London's surprise visit.

Mom let out a heavy sigh. "At least that's over."

"Agreed."

"How does Michelle feel about this?"

"I think she's okay now. We're focusing on us and our future."

"I can't wait until Sunday. Do you want to stay for dinner tonight?"

Logan stood. "No, because I need to run a few errands now. But thanks for the invite."

She got to her feet and pecked him on the cheek. "You're doing a great job on TV, by the way. So proud of you."

"You watch me?"

"Yes. Of course. You're our favorite evening news anchor."

Logan's heart swelled. "Thanks. That means a lot." He hugged her. "You're the best, Mom."

Mom hugged him back. "Love you, son."

"I love you too."

Logan parted ways and waved goodbye before exiting the house. He slipped into the driver's seat of his car and turned on his ignition. This talk with Mom gave him renewed hope in humanity. He was grateful his parents were accepting of Michelle, and he was determined to take Mom's advice and treat Marcel with kindness until he saw that he was the best man for his sister.

Logan said a prayer and drove out of his parents' neighborhood. Michelle meeting his parents was the first step into his long-term goal for their relationship. Michelle was the woman he wanted to marry. But he wouldn't rush things. Logan grimaced as he realized his most major roadblock to romance—Michelle's brother. What could he do to convince him he was a good guy?

God, show me a way.

Chapter 27

Michelle sat on the couch in her parents' home and pored over the photography from her multicultural clients' wedding. The bride was from India, and the groom was Puerto Rican.

The couple had an elaborate, beautiful wedding complete with a reception that showcased both of their cultures. For the reception, the bride changed out of her wedding dress into a blue and marigold sari. The groom wore a sherwani wedding suit that was marigold and red. They entered the reception to music from the bride's homeland and danced with their bridal party. The food was a mix of Indian and Puerto Rican dishes like chicken curry, tandoori, flan, and mango lassi beverages.

Her stomach rumbled. She wished she were still at the wedding, so she could enjoy the food. She'd been so busy capturing their love in pictures she'd forgotten to eat.

She placed her laptop on the couch, stood, and stretched. Once in the kitchen, she opened the refrigerator and pulled out a day-old carton of Chinese take-out. The scent of orange chicken over fried rice sent her stomach growling again. Taking that as confirmation, she poured it onto a plate and opened the microwave. Five minutes later, she sat at the kitchen table, satisfying her hunger.

Halfway through her midnight meal, her cell rang. Juliana. Michelle picked up the phone. "Hey, girl."

"Amiga! Is this too late to talk?"

Michelle dipped her fork into the fried rice. "No. Call me anytime, literally, and I'll answer."

"Oh, amiga. Another one of those nights?"

Michelle spoke between mouthfuls of food. "You know it."

"What's the problem this time?"

"My clients."

"They're great, no?"

"Yes, they are wonderful, but their beautiful love is not gracing the covers of our mainstream wedding magazines. I would have thought with all of my international success, by now this would not be an issue."

"My boss put your clients on her magazine cover."

"Yes, she did, and I thank you for letting God use you to help me accomplish that goal. But Jules, I want this to be a regular thing, not a flash in the pan."

"I know. I'm so sorry. What can I do to help?"

Michelle paused. "Pray about it and help me network with magazine editors."

"Will do. How are you and Logan?"

163

Michelle's cheeks warmed. "We're great. I'm going to meet his parents this weekend."

"Oh, all the feels. So happy for you."

Michelle yawned. "Yeah. Thanks."

"Have you tried pitching your photos to other mainstream wedding magazines?"

"Been there. Done that. But no call backs."

"There has to be a way around this. I'm going to pray on this for you, and we're going to trust God to make a way. You're my favorite wedding photographer not because you're my best friend but because your work is wonderful. You really know how to capture a couple's love in pictures."

"Thanks, girl."

"Anytime. Now the question is, who will be your wedding photographer?"

Michelle stifled a yawn. "What do you mean? I'm not getting married."

"You're not getting married yet, but it's only a matter of time before Logan proposes."

"How can you be so sure?"

"Um, because I think he might be the one for you."

Michelle's heart warmed. "How do you know that?"

"Because I've never seen you happier. True love looks good on you."

A smile tugged at the corner of Michelle's lips.

"And I can hear you grin through the phone."

Michelle laughed. "You got me there, amiga."

"I want to be your maid of honor."

"Girl, relax. He hasn't proposed. We've only been dating a short time."

"Yeah, but when you know, you know."

Michelle pondered Juliana's words.

"Miche?"

Juliana's voice broke her out of her silent reverie. "Yes?"

"I have to go now. I am about to crash. Good night, amiga."

"Good night, Jules."

Michelle placed her phone on the table and picked up her plate of food. She savored every bite while her mind replayed Juliana's words. Was it true that when you knew you just knew? What would become of her and Logan? Were they really headed to the altar? Only time would tell.

Her phone rang again, and her eyebrows furrowed. Annapolis Hospital. Why were they calling her?

"Hello?"

"Officer Dan Wilson calling. Is this a relative of Marcel Hadley?"

Michelle's heartbeat quickened. Was her brother okay?

"Yes, officer. I am his sister. What's the problem?"

"Your brother was in a bad car accident. He's here in Annapolis Hospital."

Her heartrate kicked up. She dropped her phone and jolted out of her seat. She grabbed the phone from the floor. "I'll be there."

~*~

Michelle burst through the hospital door and sprinted to the nurse's station. "Marcel. My brother. Is he okay?"

"What is the patient's last name?"

"Hadley."

The nurse typed on the computer. What felt like an eternity later, she peered at Michelle. "He's in the treatment room." She pointed down the hallway to her left. "Go to that door, and I'll buzz you in."

She followed directions in a hurry, only slowing out of fear of what she'd see. She took a deep breath. *Dear God, please let him be okay.*

Slowly, she pulled back the curtain.

Marcel was laid out on the hospital bed with a cast on his left leg, white gauze wrapped around his head, and a sling on his left arm. He gave her a half smile when he saw her. "Hey, sis."

She went to his bedside then gave him a hug.

"Are you okay?"

He shrugged then winced. "Been better."

"What happened?"

"A car t-boned my car. The driver was distracted. My car went spinning down the beltway. By the grace of God, it wasn't rush hour, so I managed not to hit another car or have another car hit me. God allowed my car to crash into the shoulder of the road before stopping."

"Oh, Marcel. I'm so glad you're still alive."

Marcel grimaced.

"What?"

"You may want to sit down for this."

Michelle eased into a nearby chair and gave Marcel her full attention.

"Officer Dan Wilson was the first to respond to the accident."

"Officer Dan Wilson? The same man who

called me on the phone to tell me you were here?"

Marcel raised an eyebrow. "He called you?"

Michelle nodded.

"He was the first to arrive on the scene. He called the ambulance and gave me a police escort to the hospital. He asked for my phone, but I didn't know he'd call you. I thought he'd call Mercedes. But then again, I was going in and out of consciousness, so yeah."

Michelle barely breathed. "I'm so sorry, Marcel."

Marcel looked away. "I didn't know if the accident was going to kill me. It all happened so fast, and I now know what people mean when they say that their life flashed before their eyes."

"Oh, Marcel."

"And I realized something. I don't want to die still mad at white people for the things they've done to black people and other people of color."

Michelle's breath caught in her throat. Was he saying what she thought he was saying?

"Not all white people are bad and not all white people's ancestors owned slaves and not all of them think I'm bad just because I'm black."

Michelle gave a slow nod.

Marcel took a deep breath. "And I realize I need to give Logan a fair shake."

Michelle covered her mouth, and her eyes misted. Was God really answering her prayers? Was he really softening her brother's heart and helping him see things in a more positive light? Was he really healing Marcel from the deep race-related wounds that made him so mad?

She rushed to Marcel's bedside and gave him a hug, trying not to touch his injured left side. "I'm so happy for you, bro! Praise God!"

"Yeah. It wasn't easy, but I figured it's worth it."

Michelle just hugged her brother, wanting to savor this moment.

Marcel cleared his throat. "Miche? I can't breathe."

"Sorry." She wiped the tears from her eyes. "I'm just so happy you're okay and you're going to give him a chance."

"So, when do you want me to meet the love of your life again? On better terms this time."

"As soon as possible."

"I figured you would say that."

The curtain to the cubicle parted. "Sorry to interrupt, but I wanted to make sure Marcel is okay before I leave."

Michelle whirled around to see a white police officer dressed in a blue and black uniform. She turned to her brother, who smiled at the cop.

"Yeah, I'm good. Thanks for being there for me today."

The officer nodded. "It's all in a day's work. Is this the Michelle that I called?"

"Yes, sir. I am his sister. Thanks for calling me."

"Nice to meet you." Officer Wilson turned to Marcel. "Wishing you all the best. Recover soon."

"Yes, sir."

"You can call me Dan."

"Thanks again, Dan."

The officer gave a final nod before leaving.

Michelle turned to her brother, her mouth agape. "Wow. You're really serious about this, aren't you? I like this new and improved Marcel."

He shrugged. "I'm telling you, Miche. Life and death situations will do that to you."

Michelle paused before jumping slightly.

"What?"

"Where's your phone?"

Marcel pointed to the left. "On that chair with my wallet."

She reached for it. "We need to call your wife and tell her you're okay. We need to call Mom and Dad too."

Marcel shook his head.

"What?"

"You've always been the one to keep everyone on their toes."

Michelle tilted her head. "I'll take that as a compliment."

"Yeah." He leaned his back, resting against the pillow. "Excuse me while I snooze. These painkillers are real. Wake me up when the doctor comes to tell me how long I've got to wear this cast and arm sling."

Michelle touched Marcel's right shoulder. "As long as it takes you to heal."

He didn't respond. He'd already gone to sleep.

Michelle phoned Mercedes first. She picked up after two rings.

"What's good, sis?"

Michelle looked at the dozing Marcel before responding. First, she'd tell Mercedes that Marcel

was okay then share his new lease on life.
   "Sis, you won't believe this…"

Chapter 28

Bright rays of sunlight streamed through the windows of Michelle's bedroom, waking her from her slumber. She groaned and pulled the covers over her head. Why was it so hot? Her head throbbed, her throat was sore, and she had a cough she could not shake.

She jolted and sat up straight in bed. No. Today was the day she was supposed to meet Logan's parents for dinner. Another groan. She felt miserable and not in the mood for company.

She dialed Logan's number and waited. He picked up on the fourth ring. "Hey, beautiful."

She couldn't even smile. "Hey." She grimaced at her sore throat.

"What's wrong, babe? You sound miserable."

Michelle croaked. "I'm sick."

"I'm sorry. Looks like we'd better reschedule dinner."

"Yeah." She coughed.

Logan's voice sounded like calming waters.

"Your health is our first priority, babe. We can have dinner another day."

"Aw, thanks."

"Do you like chicken noddle soup?"

"Yeah."

"Good. I'll swing by your house later on this evening. Text me your address."

"I don't want you to get sick."

"I won't stay long. Just drop off the soup. And I promise not to kiss you. Unless you want me to."

"You need to stay healthy."

"Okay. See you soon."

After ending the call, she texted Logan then fell back on her pillows. Hopefully, the doctor could see her today.

~*~

Logan stood outside of Michelle's house and shuffled his feet. How would her parents receive him, if they were even home? Just as Logan reached to ring the doorbell for a second time, the door swung open to reveal a beautiful woman, an older version of Michelle.

"Hey, Mrs. Hadley. I'm—"

"Logan. Yes, we know." Mrs. Hadley hugged him. "It's so nice to finally meet you."

Her warm embrace put his nerves at ease. "Thanks. It's an honor to meet you."

Mrs. Hadley ushered him inside. "I can see why Michelle swoons over you. You're quite the catch."

The sound of music he'd never heard before reached his ears—tropical, unique, and beautiful. The sounds were like glasses filled with water being played with a spoon. He couldn't figure out the type of music it was or what instrument the musicians were playing. "Hey, that music. What is it?"

Mrs. Hadley beamed. "Steel band. It's pretty popular in my husband's home, the island of Barbados. Do you like it?"

"It's beautiful and relaxing." "Just like living on an island." Mrs. Hadley reached for the big brown paper bag that Logan cradled in his arms. "Is this the chicken noodle soup?"

Logan nodded as he let Mrs. Hadley take the heavy bag. "My mom's recipe."

"Follow me to the kitchen and have a seat. I'll warm the soup for Michelle."

Logan obeyed orders. The scent of apples and cinnamon filled the air. "That smells so good."

Once in the kitchen, Mrs. Hadley took the soup from the bag. "I'm baking apple pie. My mom's recipe."

"Moms have the best recipes."

"I agree." She retrieved a pot from the cupboards and poured the soup into it. As she moved about the kitchen, it was clear she loved to cook. Minutes later, she sat down across the table from him. "So, tell me about yourself. Michelle gushes about you quite often, but there's nothing like hearing about you from you."

Logan and Mrs. Hadley shared a laugh.

"What would you like to know?"

"Tell me what you love about my daughter and why."

Logan cleared his throat. "I... I... W-w-well." He gazed at the ceiling and said a silent prayer. *Please God, not now*. When he gained the courage to make eye contact with Mrs. Hadley, her mocha eyes were filled with compassion.

She spoke in a gentle tone. "It's okay, Logan. Michelle told me. But I'm proud of the way you've overcome your obstacles. I watch you anchor the evening news every night."

A sigh of relief escaped Logan. "Thanks, Mrs. H-h-hadley. That m-m-means a lot." He blew out a frustrated breath. Just when he thought he had his stuttering under control, it showed up.

"Don't ever feel pressure to not stutter around Michelle and me and her dad. We accept you as you are. Don't ever be afraid to be you. We're not expecting you to be perfect."

Logan tapped his right foot. "Thanks. Where is Michelle's dad?"

"He's at work."

"On the weekend?"

Mrs. Hadley nodded. "My husband is a medical technologist. He works in the blood bank at the hospital in Bethesda on the weekends. Sometimes he has Sundays off. But normally he has to work."

"I'd like to meet him."

Mrs. Hadley didn't hide the knowing look on her face. "I know. You will." She then stood and dished out the soup. On a tray, she put the soup and a glass of orange juice. "Want to follow me to Michelle's room?"

Logan rose to his feet. "Yes. I'd love to see her."

They made their way up the stairs and to her room. Mrs. Hadley stopped at the door. "Honey, Logan is here, and we have soup for you. Can we come in?"

Michelle croaked. "Sure."

They entered, and Mrs. Hadley arranged the tray on Michelle's lap. "Feeling any better?"

"Trying to. Thanks, Mom."

"The decongestant will kick in soon. You'll be better before you know it. I'll leave you two to talk." She closed the door behind her.

Logan gazed at his girlfriend. Her hair was tousled, and her face was flushed, but to him, she was still beautiful. "Hey, gorgeous."

Michelle grimaced. "I don't feel gorgeous."

"You're always attractive to me."

Michelle chortled then winced.

Logan's heart went out to her. He sat in the chair at the desk near her bed. "That soup is known for making sick people better after a few servings. It's my mom's special recipe."

Michelle dipped her spoon into the soup and slurped it. "This tastes good. Your mom can cook."

"I made it at Mom's house earlier today using her recipe."

"You can cook like this?"

Logan grinned. "Yeah."

"I may just have to marry you."

"I share that sentiment."

A blush graced her face. She continued eating. Even when she was sick, she was graceful.

"Don't you have plans for today?"

Logan shook his head. "My only plans for today were to visit you and help you get better."

Her eyes welled with tears. "Aw, really?"

He spoke softly. "Yes, babe. I love you."

Michelle cried. "I love you too."

He went to her and kissed her temple.

"I can't promise you won't get sick by getting this close."

"I'm willing to take that risk."

Moments later, she slurped the last of the soup. She turned to Logan. "That was the best chicken noodle soup I've ever eaten."

"Happy to hear that."

"I'm sorry I'm too sick to meet your parents tonight."

"It's okay. We can reschedule."

Michelle yawned.

Logan reached for her tray. "Why don't you get some sleep? I'll take this to your mom in the kitchen."

"Thanks, babe." She laid down and snuggled beneath her bed covers. Before he could say another word, she'd dozed off.

He smiled then leaned down and kissed her forehead. "Sweet dreams, love."

As he walked down the hallway then down the stairs, his heart swelled. He knew now what he'd felt before. Michelle was going to be his wife. He just had to ask her dad for his blessing and propose. He prayed for God to show him the right time.

"All done?"

Mrs. Hadley's voice jolted Logan out of his private thoughts. "Yes ma'am." He handed her the tray.

Mrs. Hadley accepted the tray and set it on the kitchen table. "You're welcome to stay for dinner. Michelle's father should be home by then."

Was it too soon to ask her dad for his blessing? If he stayed, this could be the perfect opportunity. "I'd love to."

Chapter 29

It was a beautiful, warm evening graced by cool breezes. Michelle and Logan had just arrived at his parents' house and sat in his cobalt-blue Porsche as Michelle took in the beauty in the sprawling, lush green estate. It was the most beautiful in the gated community. Maybe it was because Logan grew up here that made it special. But maybe the circular driveway and gorgeous golden brick front with deep blue shutters on the windows of the stately mansion also played a part in captivating Michelle's heart.

They strolled up the pink rose-bush bordered pathway toward the front door. Logan held her right hand, and Michelle used her left hand to straighten her royal blue blouse and adjust her black pencil skirt. She ran a hand through her hair and smiled at its butter smoothness thanks to the natural blowout her hair stylist had given her earlier today.

Logan leaned in. "You look beautiful." He kissed her temple, and she almost swooned. "Just be yourself. My parents already love you."

He gave her hand a reassuring squeeze, and her heart swelled. She kissed his cheek. "I hope so."

Logan cupped her chin and turned her toward him. "I know so." He kissed her lips, and her heart performed somersaults.

Before she could say a word, the door swung open. Isabella greeted them with a wide smile and a big hug. "*Señor* Logan! So happy to see you and *tu novia.*"

Logan whispered to Michelle. "She said you're my girlfriend."

"I know. I recognized that word."

Logan faced Isabella. *"Hola! Cómo estás?"*

"*Estoy bien.*" Isabella stepped aside. "*Que linda*! Please, come in."

Logan translated again. "She said you're very pretty."

"*Gracias.*"

"*De nada,*" Isabella replied. "*Señor y Señora* Emerson are waiting for you in the dining room."

Michelle elbowed Logan. "Are we late?"

"No. My parents are just very prompt."

Logan and Michelle followed Isabella to the elaborate dining room. A woman with luxurious, long, honey-brown hair and clear skin turned from facing a man of regal stature and smiled at Logan. "Hey, honey." She stood.

"Hi, Mom! Dad."

The man stood tall and appeared a bit stoic. "Son."

Mrs. Emerson walked toward Michelle. "You must be Michelle." Mrs. Emerson embraced her in a warm hug that calmed her nerves. "It's so good to meet you."

Her warm welcome made Michelle feel at home. She returned the hug. "You too."

"Please, have a seat. Logan, your father and I were just discussing how happy we are for you in your career and in your relationship with this lovely lady."

Michelle's cheeks warmed. Logan held out a chair, and she slipped into it. He then walked around the table and sat in the chair across from her.

"Thanks, Mom. God's blessed me on my job, and Michelle does make me very happy."

Michelle blushed. Mrs. Emerson smiled. "I see."

"Michelle."

She turned to Mr. Emerson. "Yes, sir?"

"Please, call me Ryan. It's nice to meet you."

"Thanks, sir. I mean Ryan. It's nice to meet you too."

Mrs. Emerson leaned in. "And you can call me April. We're having rack of lamb for dinner. Do you like it well-done?"

No sooner than Mrs. Emerson spoke, a man dressed in a traditional chef's uniform and top hat entered the room. Two young women dressed in knee-length black pencil skirts and short-sleeved white blouses followed him. They each carried platters of food and took turns placing it on the table. At the enticing aroma, Michelle's taste buds watered. Rack of lamb served with a rosemary sauce, couscous with dates, and a green salad with feta cheese and vinaigrette dressing. "This looks and smells delicious, April."

"Thank you."

The chef and waiters served dinner while Michelle got to know Logan's parents. She bit into the savory lamb and a heavenly food symphony struck a chord in her mouth. She dipped her spoon into the couscous and enjoyed the deliciousness before picking up her fork and sampling the fresh green salad with feta cheese. Delightful. "I've never had a better meal. Your chefs are talented. Are they from a five-star restaurant?"

Mrs. Emerson nodded. "Yes, and they are classically trained."

"That's wonderful."

"So, Michelle," Ryan said. "Logan says you're a wedding photographer. How did you get into that career?"

"I've always had a passion for photography. Gratefully, God blessed me with parents who wanted me to follow my creative career dreams."

Ryan nodded. "Logan says you live with your parents?"

"Yes. They're letting me stay home while I build my business."

"And about how long will that take?"

Logan interjected. "Dad."

"No, it's okay." She turned to Ryan. "I'm almost done and will have enough money to move into my own house within a year. God's really blessed my business in both the studio I own and my own work as a wedding photographer. My first international wedding really helped."

Ryan raised his eyebrows. "Where was that?"

"Italy."

"Impressive. How did it help your career?"

"It opened the door for me to have my photography featured on the covers of notable international wedding magazines."

"Sounds lovely," Mrs. Emerson said.

"Do you not have exposure here in America?"

Logan sighed. "Dad."

"Yes, I do. My studio is a success, and my clients have been on the cover of one American wedding magazine, but I want to see more of my clients grace the covers of mainstream bridal magazines here in the USA."

Ryan turned his attention to Logan. "She's a woman of ambition. Good catch, son."

Logan's shoulders relaxed. "Thanks, Dad."

Relief washed over Michelle too. It looked like Logan's parents both liked her.

After talking and eating dinner, April pushed her plate back. "I hope you eat dessert, dear. So many girls these days are watching their figures."

April had a flawless figure. If she delved into dessert on a daily basis, it didn't show. "I love sweets."

"Good. We have crème brûlée."

"My favorite."

Moments later, the waiters served dessert. Michelle dipped her spoon into the crème brûlée, cracking its shell of sugar and glaze and delving deep into the creamy texture. She closed her eyes and savored the delight. When she opened her eyes, Logan and his parents were holding back their grins. Heat rose to her cheeks. So embarrassing. "I'm sorry. It just tastes delicious." They laughed. It felt more like a family dinner than meeting Logan's parents, and she cherished that feeling, holding it close to her heart.

After dessert and closing their conversation that had lasted for hours, Logan helped Michelle out of her chair. He kissed his mother's cheek and gave both her and his dad a hug as he said goodbye. He then turned to Michelle and touched her lower back. "Ready to go?"

Michelle nodded. Logan turned to his parents again. "Thanks for your hospitality, Mom and Dad. Hopefully, we can do this again."

"It would be our pleasure," Ryan said. "Your Michelle already feels like part of our family."

Her heart leapt. What a high compliment.

"I agree. She does feel like family." Logan kissed her.

Rainfall greeted them when they stepped outside. She instinctively reached up to shield her hair. Logan took off his jacket and held it over her head. "Don't worry, my love. You're sweet, but you're not sugar. The rain won't melt you."

"Maybe not, but it will morph my straight hair into an abundance of curls."

"I think curly hair is adorable so in that case…" He removed his jacket.

"No, I need that covering."

He raced in front of her, and she ran to catch up him. All the while, the rain wet her hair. Should she be mad because she just got a blow out or happy because Logan made her laugh?

When she finally caught up with him, he was standing by his car with a teasing smile. "What took you so long?"

Michelle caught her breath. "You run fast."

"And you look very adorable with curly hair."

Michelle touched her hair, now curly from the rain. "Logan, I just straightened it."

"And what does that matter? You look gorgeous with your hair straight or curly. It's a win-win." Logan's eyes danced. "Now, come here and kiss me."

She walked into his arms and gazed into the depths of his ocean-blue eyes. "Just when I thought nothing could compare to the beautiful, deep, clear water of the Caribbean islands, God created all that and more in your eyes."

He drew her in and kissed her, and for a moment in time, she didn't care about the rain or her hair. All she cared about was him. The warmth of his embrace, the tenderness and passion of his lips on hers, and the way that being with him made her heart swell with happiness. She'd met her husband. She was sure of it. Now when would he propose?

Chapter 30

"I really don't understand why you're insisting on doing my makeup today, Jules. You know I don't like wearing a lot of cake on my face."

Juliana bit her bottom lip, and Michelle cast a look at her in the mirror. One she recognized. There was something Juliana wasn't telling her. "What's going on?"

Juliana avoided eye contact. She dipped her makeup brush into the blush. "Nothing. Relax. I just want you to look pretty for your date with Logan tonight."

Michelle studied Juliana for a moment. Well, she'd trust her. She stilled so that Juliana could apply her blush then liquid eyeliner.

"How is he? Logan."

"More wonderful every time I see him. I met his parents last weekend over dinner at their dream-worthy mansion."

Juliana's hand stilled. "Mansion?"

"Yes, they live in Potomac. Their home is

something you only see in the movies. They have an Olympic-sized indoor pool, a theater that's large enough to seat a hundred people, and a dining room so expansive I was tempted to text everyone at the table instead of talk. Yet everything about their home was so warm, welcoming, and very cozy."

Juliana tilted her head. "Really? Wow." After she finished the eyeliner, she reached for the lip liner and gloss. She paused. "Lipstick or lip gloss?"

Michelle shot Juliana a look. "I'm a lip gloss girl. You know that."

"Yes. I do." Juliana reached for a beautiful rose-pink gloss and the lip liner that was a shade darker. She drew the liner on Michelle's lips then glossed her lips with color. She handed a mirror to Michelle. "You're all done, beautiful."

Michelle gazed at her reflection. She resembled a magazine cover model. "You made me gorgeous."

Juliana waved. "Amiga, you're already gorgeous. I just enhanced your look."

Michelle hugged Juliana. "I'd love to stay, but I need to go home and change."

"Understood. I do miss our times together."

"You're right. We haven't had many girl days or girl talks because I've been so busy with work and Logan. I'm sorry. Let's schedule a meet-up for next week."

"I'd like that."

Michelle grabbed her purse and went to the door. Juliana followed. "Wear the red dress."

Michelle turned around. Last night, she'd texted a picture of her brand-new dress with a sweetheart neckline and sleek material that accentuated her curves and stopped at her knees. She'd planned to wear it to dinner next time he took her to one of his favorite fancy restaurants. "Why? We're just having dinner on Logan's boat."

Juliana crossed her arms. "Trust me on this. You'll thank me later."

Why was Juliana being so secretive? "I demand you tell me what's going on."

Juliana pushed Michelle out the door. "Go! Don't be late for your date."

That was odd.

Once outside, the cool breeze combed through her just-straightened hair, and the sunlight kissed her face.

For a moment, she basked in the sun before slipping into the driver's seat of her car. There was only one way to find out what Logan had planned. She had to meet him. Why did she feel like tonight was the start of something special? Great anticipation pumped through her vessels as she drove. Could this be the night that led to greater things?

~*~

Logan greeted Michelle as she wandered down the slip to his boat. He extended a hand and helped her climb on deck then took her in his arms and kissed her cheek. "Hello, beautiful." She wore a red dress and black heels. Her hands clutched a red purse, and her hair rested on her shoulders in a natural, straight look. He gazed into her golden-brown eyes. "You are my lady in red, and you look gorgeous."

A soft blush graced Michelle's face. "Thanks,

love."

"Have a seat. We're going to sail out tonight."

He undid the rope and pulled the anchor before setting sail. Moments later, they were in the middle of the water, watching the sunset. The water ebbed and flowed, and the boat rocked ever so slightly. They lay back on the couch on the open deck, watching the stars fill the sky. Michelle sighed. "This is beautiful."

"No more beautiful than you."

Michelle swatted his arm. "Aren't you the smooth talker tonight?"

Logan propped himself on his arm. "Hey. I call it like I see it."

Michelle pursed her lips. Her eyes shone like the stars in the sky. He kissed her then reached for her hand. "Come on." He pulled her to her feet then pressed a remote control and the song "Waiting for A Girl Like You" by Foreigner played. He drew her close, and they swayed to the music. "I've been waiting for a girl like you."

She melted into his arms. "I've been waiting for a man like you."

Logan released her. "Well then that settles it." His heart pounding, he dropped to one knee and reached into his pocket. He retrieved a small velvet box and popped it open. "Michelle Hadley, you are the one woman that my heart loves like no other. Every moment we spend together makes me want to know you better, hold you closer, and grow old with you."

He cleared his throat. "What I'm trying to s-s-say is…" He paused inhaled. "Michelle, will you marry me?"

Michelle nodded. His hands shook as he slipped the ring on her finger.

"Yes, I'll marry you." She turned it so it caught the dying sun's rays. "I love it. But even without a ring, I love you."

He rose to his feet and drew her in for a kiss. "I'm happy to hear that, but the ring is yours to keep. I'll give you an even better one on our wedding day."

She kissed his face repeatedly, and he laughed. "I feel the same way."

"I love you, Logan Emerson."

"And I love you, Michelle Hadley. Soon to be Michelle Emerson."

They sealed their engagement with another kiss. Michelle's stomach rumbled, interrupting their embrace. Logan gave half a chuckle. "Ready for dinner, fiancée?"

"I'm ready for dinner and the rest of our lives together, forever."

He took her hands in his and led her into the inner lounge area of his boat where they shared dinner and looked at each other with a twinkle in their eyes that was only rivaled by the bright stars in the sky.

Epilogue

One year later

The song "Endless Love" played in the background as Michelle walked down the aisle in her wedding gown with her dad by her side. The song could only begin to describe what her heart felt for Logan. Today marked the first day of what she dreamed would be a lifetime of happiness together, and the location for their wedding ceremony made their day even more special. They had chosen Ravello on Italy's Amalfi Coast because Michelle fell in love with it when she shot her first international wedding.

The view was spectacular. Colorful houses and deep blue water left the entire setting tranquil and serene. The scent of the ceremony's floral gardens wafted on the cool ocean breeze that teased her curly hair.

Hopefully, she and Logan would have time together on the coast before going back home. They had seven days after their nuptials to explore this romantic destination together as husband and wife.

Nico snapped photos of her on the bridal pathway. Mom, Marcel, and Mercedes sat in the front row as she approached the altar. Marcel smiled, and Mercedes gave her a thumbs-up.

Over the past year, between her prayers, Mercedes's heart-to-heart talks with Marcel, and the car accident that almost claimed his life, he learned how to deal with his mistrust of white people. He gave Logan a fair shake and apologized for his behavior. It helped that, after the engagement, there were moments where Marcel saw how much Logan loved her, and her brother softened. With the whole family here and happy, it was more than she could ask.

They arrived at the front, and the pastor opened his book. "Who gives this woman in marriage today?"

In a deep baritone voice, her dad answered, "I do." He turned to Michelle and kissed her cheek. He gave her hands a reassuring squeeze. Michelle mouthed, "Thank you." He joined Mom in the seats.

As Michelle picked up her dress to climb the two steps, Juliana rushed to adjust her train.

Michelle's hands trembled a little bit as she met Logan's gaze. The love in his eyes melted her heart. He reached out and grasped her hands. They shared a moment, and in that moment, his touch and loving gaze calmed her nerves. Together, they turned to the pastor.

He greeted their guests, shared his kind thoughts about Michelle and Logan, read from the Bible, and then asked for the wedding bands. Logan and Michelle took turns repeating the key words, "Thee I do wed," as they slipped their rings on each other's fingers.

Then came the moment Michelle had waited for her entire life. "I now pronounce you husband and wife. Logan, you may kiss your bride."

He cradled her face then drew her into a romantic, sweet, and passionate kiss that had her knees going soft. The crowd shouted for joy.

"I now introduce to you Mr. and Mrs. Emerson."

They held hands and faced their guests. Her heart skipped a beat when he scooped her in his arms and carried her down the platform and down the aisle. She looped her arms around his neck. "Always ready to sweep me off my feet, aren't you?"

He planted a kiss on her lips. "Always. This is just the beginning." They reached the spot where Nico told them to wait so he could get post-nuptial photos. Logan set Michelle down. They held hands and just gazed at each other for a moment until a familiar voice interrupted.

"*Bella* Michelle."

Nico ran toward her with a broad grin on his face and his Canon DSLR camera in his hands. He hugged her and kissed her cheeks. He then gave Logan a bear hug that almost toppled her groom.

"I am happy for you two lovebirds. God is good, no?"

"Yes, Nico," Michelle responded. "He is."

Nico raised his hands. "*Molto bella*!"

He then gestured to the shore. "Follow me. We take pictures here then by the water, no?"

Logan nodded. "Anything for you, my beautiful bride. I'm happy you're my wife."

"And I'm happy you're my husband."

He dipped her and kissed her as Nico captured the moment on camera. They then followed him to their next location, so he could capture their love in pictures. What a beautiful day, one they would always remember and treasure forever.

~ The End ~

Keep reading for the first chapter of *A Second Chance.*

Author Bio:

Alexis A. Goring is a writer at heart who loves the arts!

She followed her passion for the Arts & Entertainment industry in school, earning a B.A. in Print Journalism and an MFA in Creative Writing.

She's established as an author, blogger, editor, writer, and photographer who enjoys exploring matters of the heart in her work.

Alexis has worked as the Growing Up columnist for Collegiate Quarterly (CQ), editor of a newspaper in the West, and she is the founder of a mission-focused blog called "God is Love."

She enjoys interviewing people, eating good food, listening to beautiful music, watching great movies, visiting bookstores, and shopping.

Love in Pictures is her second book published by Forget Me Not Romances.

Alexis hopes that her writing will connect readers with the forever love of Jesus Christ. She is a member of American Christian Fiction Writers (ACFW) and Romance Writers of America (RWA).

Readers can learn more about Alexis and can connect with her online via her official website, https://alexisagoring.jimdo.com.

A Second Chance

Chapter 1

Knee-deep in debt from wedding expenses, Traci Hightower sighed as she filed through the credit card statements. She should be married now, back from her honeymoon in Bali, and settled into her new home with her husband.

Happy.

Not single and broke.

She slapped an envelope against the desk. Five months of struggling to survive and pay off the debt. Her meager, entry-level journalist salary didn't stretch far enough. She'd been paying her dues for seven years. She rubbed her temples. The numbers on the credit card statement blurred in front of her eyes.

The doorbell rang. A little thrill rushed through her. She stood from her cross-legged position on the floor and hopped over the mess of papers and laundry that decorated her living room. "Who is it?"

"The woman who gave you birth."

For the first time today, Traci smiled. She opened the

door and reached for a hug from the one person who never left her hanging. "Hi, Mom."

Her mom returned her daughter's embrace, then dragged her suitcase inside. She glanced around. "Oh, my."

Traci locked her door, then turned and shrugged. "I'm so glad you're here. I've been looking forward to this. Can't you stay for more than two days though?"

Mom stopped picking up the bills from the floor and faced her daughter. "No, honey. I'm sorry, but I need to return home by Wednesday morning. Dad and I have an important meeting later that day."

Traci's heart dipped. Mom paused and placed the bills and the stack of paper she'd picked off the floor on Traci's kitchen counter. "Oh, sweetie." She cocooned her daughter in another embrace.

Traci snuggled close. She inhaled the familiar scent of her mother's favorite perfume. It smelt like coconut and lime.

"You always were a cuddler." Mom stroked her hair. "Still up to your eyeballs in debt?"

Traci nodded.

"Why don't you let me and your father help?"

Traci took a step back and made eye contact with her mom. "We've been through this. I got myself into this mess. I'll get myself out."

Mom smiled. "Your father and I were talking. We hate to see you struggling."

"You don't exactly live in a palace either. I know you want to retire soon, and I won't have you dipping into that money."

Mom reached into her purse. "Living in the nation's capital area is expensive." She rummaged through her handbag's contents. "Have you considered moving home?"

"I can't do that. I don't ever want to live anywhere

else. My life and career are here."

"How's that going for you?"

Traci picked at her fingernails. "It could be better." Better boss, better pay, better office space. The works.

Mom nodded as she retrieved one sealed envelope from her purse. She looked toward Traci's kitchen. "Can we make some tea? I'd like to talk with you."

"Sure. Come with me." Traci reached for the box of peppermint tea bags and got a bottle of honey from her refrigerator. As she put the kettle on to boil, her mom settled into a wobbly kitchen chair. She smoothed the creased edges of the envelope.

Traci poured the hot water over the tea bags in each mug and the scent of peppermint filled the air. "Everything okay?"

"Just thinking, honey."

"About what?"

"Have a seat."

"Sure, just let me allow the tea to steep." After she placed a plate over each mug and set it aside, she settled into the chair across from her mom. "What's up?"

"I never did like Greg."

Traci traced a ring stain on the table. "Do we have to talk about my ex-fiancé?"

"Yes, because your grandfather always trusted my judgment."

"So, Grandpa didn't like Greg either?"

"I inherited my instincts of discernment from him. Speaking of discernment, here." She pushed the envelope within Traci's reach.

She frowned as she picked it up and tried to flatten its wrinkles. "What's this?"

"Open it. Read it, and I'll bring our tea to the table."

Traci turned over the letter-sized, manila-hued paper that was addressed to her. She drew out the paper.

Dear Traci,

If you're reading this, it means I've passed away, and your mother kept her promise to give this to you at the right time. As you know, I like to cut to the chase first and explain later. So here it is, plain and simple: I left an inheritance for you. It's enough for you to make a solid and secure living, for it will cover more than what you need for the rest of your life.

Traci dropped the letter, her hands shaking. This could be the answer to her financial struggles and give her what she always dreamed of. Her own bookstore. The thought stole her breath for a moment. She envisioned the words on the sign out front. Hallee's House. Just like she promised her cousin Hallee before she passed away from cancer. Tears welled in Traci's eyes.

Forcing herself to take a deep breath and will the emotional waterworks away, she picked the paper off the floor and continued reading.

But you cannot receive the money until after you are married, and before you are, your mother must approve of the man you want to wed. Why? Because your mother inherited my sense of judgment and discernment between right and wrong when it comes to people. She can spot someone who's going to break your heart from a mile away. I trust that you will listen to your mother now that I'm gone and can no longer advise you. So there you have it, dear. You have an inheritance. Sounds like a movie, right? Only it's not. It's better, because it's now part of the story of your life.

After you're married, you and your husband need to visit my lawyer, Chadwick Morrison. Provide him with the original copy of your marriage certificate, and he will give you your inheritance.

Your grandmother and I loved you. We wanted nothing more than for you to find the type of love that we had during our lifetime. Now, I trust that you will allow yourself to be guided by God, your mother's love, and your father's protection.

With love, your grandfather,
Henry Allen Fort

P.S. Take this seriously. Don't marry the wrong man just to get the money. Let love happen. There's no deadline. My will said you had to be married first. It didn't say when.

"Let love happen." Traci snorted as she folded the letter and placed it into the envelope. "The last time I let love happen, I was left at the altar with nothing more than a pile of bills."

Mom placed her mug on the table. "It's time for you to move on and trust God."

"I trusted God to bring me a husband. He brought me Greg. Remember? The man who left me on my wedding day and ran off with my best friend?"

"Honey, I know it hurts, but that was months ago. You shouldn't allow Greg's actions and wayward heart to tarnish your future. Be glad he showed you his true colors before tying the knot. Honestly, look at this as a blessing. God protected you from a lifetime of heartache."

Traci focused on her I Love Maryland mug.

Mom touched her hand. "Your grandfather just wanted to see you happy in a committed romantic relationship like he and your grandma had. Like your father and I have."

Traci sipped her tea.

"Keep the letter." Mrs. Hightower pushed her chair back. "Do you want me to stay here or at a hotel?"

"Here, Mom, of course. You can stay in my room. I'll sleep on the couch."

"Alright then. I'm going to put my luggage in your room. After that, we'll clean your apartment."

Traci picked up the mugs while her mind ran a marathon. Forgive her ex-fiancé and move on? Trust God?

Impossible.

10742737R00127

Made in the USA
Lexington, KY
30 September 2018